Song of t

A Collection of Short Stories

by

Aeris Walker

ISBN: 979-8-9862976-6-8 (Paperback edition)
ISBN: 979-8-9862976-7-5 (eBook edition)

Any references to historical events, real people, or real places are used fictitiously. Names, characters, and places are products of the author's imagination.

Book design by Blue Marble Storytellers.
Artwork by Russell Norman

First printed edition 2023.
Blue Marble Publishing LLC

To my husband, Brian.

Your encouragement is like oxygen; my lungs are full.

Introduction

For the longest time, I thought of myself as a "someday writer:" maybe when the kids were older and I had more time or more experience, more knowledge of the world. Maybe once I finished *this* book or *that* book about how to write better, I would finally begin my own writing journey. But *beginning* always felt so daunting.

They say the best time to plant a tree was 20 years ago, but the second-best time is right now. I knew someday I wanted to be basking in the shade of my own "tree"—or rather shielding my face from the sun with the hardback cover of my own literary creation. This collection is the planting of that tree—the tender seedling of what I hope will flourish into something full and mature. These stories are an exploration of voice, perspective, and style. They branch across multiple genres from fantasy to historical fiction, drama to suspense. While varied and distinct, all are the fruit of one author's imagination.

Muses are flighty and unpredictable, and inspiration is so vapid. I've found that waiting for either to show up and spark ideas was a futile use of time, and so, many of these stories were written as responses to writing prompts that guided the direction or established the "essence" of the story. The prompts provided the push required to craft something fresh and original, compelling me to reach beyond what I thought were the boundaries of my own creativity.

I imagine the literary world as an ancient and thickly dense forest, where renowned writers are like great redwood trees stretching up into the sky, their roots immovable. It's a crowded place, bursting with beautiful words and big ideas—maybe some poisonous ones too. It's a place teeming with new life—fresh writers all lifting their faces toward the sun, striving for light in the shade of the giants above them, to become something not so easily squashed underfoot or withered by drought. It's an overwhelming world—a place so easy to feel small in—a world where every great tree once began as a seed.

Aeris Walker

March 2023

Contents

Song of the Forest

Music is better when it is shared.

According to the lore, Humans cannot experience the music of the forest.

At least, that's what I've always been told. They are a species of just five senses, and even those have limitations; colors appear muted, textures are nearly imperceptible under their blunted fingertips, and sounds fall flat. Apparently, their hearing abilities are so atrophied they can only discern one distinct voice in a bird's song, completely missing the three-part harmony of its chirped tune. Clearly they lack the sense of perception—I've seen it. I have watched the Humans interact with almost no acknowledgement of one another's feelings, as if they are entirely blind to the syrupy clouds of color formed by emotion which hover above their heads.

Taste must be affected too or else they'd never leave the forest, where even the moist air lights the tongue like sweet nectar. But the music—I often wonder if they'd tread differently in our woods if they could hear it. It's overwhelming at times, the sound of a million trees and insects and plants all emitting their unique chiming vibrations into time and space. The ancient oaks resonate their deep, low moan; streams bubble their crisp tenor. Dew drops sing in liquid whispers, and vibrant green ferns pulsate their erratic staccato, layering our song in anticipation.

But under every rock, plant, and fungus, spanning the endless underground, are the mycelium with their spidery threads connecting all forest life; their ultrasonic hum is easily the most beautiful sound in the universe. Their voice establishes the key in which we all sing.

My wings brush against each other in a lyrical swish, feather against feather. My kind has thrived in these forests—in nature—since the beginning of time, but the Human mind is unable to comprehend our existence and so my species remains unseen—invisible through the ages. Legend indicates we once co-existed, but in the Humans' thirst for transcendence, they advanced, scanning the stars for the universe's secrets, then bowed to mathematics with her cold logic. And when they fell in worship at the feet of science's unyielding laws, they abandoned the pursuits of the spirit realm, losing all connection to those peripheral, ethereal senses.

In their frenzied striving for omniscience, they'd unknowingly severed a limb, blinded one eye to an entire world they were *in* but no longer *of.* Now, they look at us and only see what makes sense—maybe an exotic moth or butterfly, but never the truth.

Nestled under a red-capped Amanita muscaria, I awake to the breathy sighs of infant fronds unfurling from their curled dormancy. Sunlight trickles between the trees and warms the new life as they join our song with airy, wobbly voices. A doe and her young fawn pad across the mossy forest floor, their brassy huffs wafting in the air. They stop short and jerk their heads up, silent, ears twitching, before they bolt beyond the trees in a flash of brown and white fur. I place my ear to the ground, where the mycelium hum and squeal at the pressure from an above ground visitor, somewhere beyond the stream. I flit above the bushy sedges and birch tree saplings where I see something—someone—teetering toward me. A Human. A small, squishy Human.

Her wild sprigs of hair shudder like leaves in the wind and her skin is as smooth as a river stone. A cloud of pale-pink hovers over her body—*curiosity, innocence*. She wavers on the uneven ground, plump limbs bouncing with each step. She squats and rubs a patch of moss like a house pet. Its purr is like glass bells. The Human laughs, a trickling, lilting giggle. She plucks a petal from a dainty white flower, and it gasps. The Human's eyes grow large, and she stumbles. Her aura shifts from pink to a murky gray—*uncertainty, confusion*. She bends her ear to the maimed plant and listens, listens.

Humans have traipsed and tramped through these woods for as long as I can remember, since my emergence—the day I poked and cracked my way out of that lucent chrysalis. Many wanderers have entered these woods; some are fearful, but most are searching. They are a restless species, cognizant of the void, yearning for wholeness in a grayscale world of their own design. The spirit realm whispers and pulls with its siren song, but they do not hear. Cannot hear. At least, that's what I've always been told.

This sprite of a child suggests otherwise. My hands scrape against lichen on the trunk of a monolithic redwood tree as I cling, watching. If she can hear, could she see? See me? As I have done a thousand times before, I spring from the safety of the trees and chart an intersecting path with the Human.

I encircle her crown of curls and she turns in a staggering arc, following my flight, dewy eyes locked with mine. Her dimpled hand rises, reaching, pointing, and a sound like the crystalline chiming of the Trillium flower escapes her lips when she speaks.

"Baby!"

I sputter and crash into a narrow branch, scratching my delicate cheek. Though centuries older than this child, it is natural that a Human might describe my diminutive features as infant-esque, though until now, that was only conjecture. The girl leans into the brush where I've fallen, her head tilted—watching, waiting. She claps and coos when I rise, then loses her balance and plunks onto the ground near a cluster of golden mushrooms.

She does not flinch when I flutter closer, just a heartbeat away from her pert nose. I lift one hand, she lifts one finger, and we touch—two species, two worlds, connected like searching tendrils. The mushrooms below us radiate a hollow, smooth timbre, cloaking the moment in somber warmth. My wings tingle in a rush of excitement. I fly down and rest my head near the mushrooms' spongy caps and urge the child to do the same, pointing to my ear. She lumbers onto unsteady arms and lowers herself, ear crooning toward the strumming fungi. Moisture gathers on her unparted lips.

I flit away, and hover near a beetle scuttling over strips of bark. I point to my ear again and she leans in, listening. The beetle's song is metallic, bright, notes coming in short bursts. The girl laughs and I find myself laughing with her; beetles do make quite a jaunty noise. I have never known a silent world, a world without music, but I hear each sound almost as if for the first time as I share it with the small Human—this anomaly of her species. I descend, below the exuberant foliage and plant my feet against the cool, damp earth. I point to the ground and lay down, ear to dirt.

The child mimics my actions and sprawls out along the forest floor, ear to earth. The mycelium's hum is high and clear, like wind against glassy snowflakes. Their silvery song stretches for miles in the rich soil, an underground celestial choir. The girl is still as stone, unmoving but for her lips, which tremble. Her voice is honey, smooth and mellow, as she matches the pitch of the ethereal hum–singing. The music of the forest is more beautiful than ever. Her aura is azure—a rare, dazzling blue, the color of wonder, magic. *Spirit.*

The mycelium squeal, their steady song dipping and shuddering. Footsteps, frantic and heavy, shake the forest; someone is running. I peer above a fallen tree to see a woman racing over the uneven ground, stomping grass and moss underfoot. The cloud of color above her swirls from orange to scarlet—*fear, distress, panic.* Her wild heartbeat sluices, like iron in water. She stops and turns in halting half circles, searching, calling. At the sound, the child lifts her head from the damp ground.

"Mama."

Dried leaves dangle from her hair when she rises on unsteady feet. Our eyes meet, two worlds, being pulled apart like roots from the earth. Her plump hand wiggles. *Goodbye.* She turns and rushes toward the woman, stumbling over thick growth. A rainbow of emotion explodes above the woman when she sees the child, shades of joy, relief, guilt.

Love. When they embrace, a veil of rare, dazzling blue shrouds them.

Spirit.

It is unlikely I will ever encounter the child again, and I wonder, when she has grown and assimilated into her grayscale world, if she will remember me, remember the forest. *Remember the music.*

If I Let You

Not all bribes come in the shape of dollar bills.

If I let you touch her, will you please be gentle? Just squeeze her little foot, rub her hand, feel her soft head. Look, she's smiling; she likes you.

If I let you hold her, will you please stop pouting? Here, come sit on the couch. Be gentle, not too tight—hold her head up. She's new and little, and you must be careful. This is your sister; she lives here now, and I know she's going to love you.

If I bring you your own blanket, would you please stop crying? Here, I'll wrap it around your shoulders, all soft and warm. And here's a hat for your head. Now you look just like your baby sister.

If I make you a snack, would you please settle down? Will you sit here at the table and eat your crackers, drink your juice? Your sister is hungry, and I must feed her. I know you want to help, but she is too young; she can't eat what you eat yet. But she will grow bigger and stronger, and someday you can help. You'll feed her carrots from a jar or milk from a bottle. Be patient for now. Please eat your snack.

If I take you to Grandma's house, would that make you happy? You can bake cookies together and decorate them with icing. Maybe Grandpa will let you sit in his big office chair and spin in circles. It won't be for long, just a few days.

You'll have fun, I know it. Your sister is a newborn—a brand new baby, and sometimes new babies need extra attention. But I'll see you in a few days, and I'll miss you very much.

When I pick you up from Grandma's house we can get ice cream, would you like that? We will put your sister in the stroller, and walk to the ice cream shop, and sit on the bench together outside. You must eat it quickly, or it will melt in the heat. I know you want to share, but your sister cannot have ice cream yet. Please, just eat your ice cream.

If I take you to the playground, would that help you calm down? I can push you on the swings or watch you on the slide, at least for a little while. I know how much you love the playground, but when your sister begins to fuss and cry, it will be time to go. She'll need to eat, and we still have to go to the store.

If I let you push the cart, will you please stop screaming? You cannot scream in the grocery store. I need you to stop screaming. Please stop.

If I hug you tight, will you forgive me for screaming too? Please, let's just go home.

If I give you this new toy, will you take it to your room and be a good boy? I'll put in batteries, and you can push all the buttons and see what it does. Pull it across the floor and watch each wheel go around and around. Not too loudly, please; Mommy's head hurts. Your sister cried so much last night; she's still a new baby.

If I turn on a movie for you, will you please be quiet? I know you like to be silly and loud, but your sister is finally asleep; you must be still. Anything you want, here, come and sit down. I'll bring you a blanket and your bear, and you can watch tv for a while. Mommy has so much to do. I'll come and sit with you soon. Please, just watch your movie.

If I give you this pot and this wooden spoon, would you please get out of the kitchen? Go play, just over there. It's nearly dinnertime and Mommy is trying to wash, and chop, and cook and it's so hard with you underfoot. Everything is such a mess, and now I think I hear the baby crying. Or was it only a bird? Just please, stay out of the kitchen.

When Daddy gets home, will you go to him, please? Let him take you outside or read you a book. You can show him your drawings, or go ride your bike, or pretend you're a frog and hunt for bugs in the yard—all the things I didn't have time to do with you today. Your sister is upset right now, and Mommy must help her. I know you want her to come play with you, but she is too little to ride a bike or jump like a frog. Someday she will be bigger, and you can do all those things together.

When it's time for dinner, will you just eat your food, please? No picking, or poking, or whining—just eat. Let Daddy pretend your potato is an airplane or your chicken a choo-choo-train, and open wide for them to come in. Please don't cry and complain. We've all had a long day. Just eat your dinner, it's almost time for bed.

If I bring you the boat and the yellow rubber duck, will you please stop splashing? You're getting water all over the floor, and Mommy's trying to wash your hair. There you go, just sit still. Look at all the bubbles, here on your chest, your arms. You look like a little cloud—a sleepy little cloud.

If I let you pick out your favorite pajamas, the pair with the dinosaurs dancing under palm trees, would that make you smile? I love when you smile.

If I crawl in bed with you, the bed you've nearly outgrown, will you let me hold you and tell you a story? Will you let me smell your hair and kiss your face and sing you a song?

If I tell you that things will get easier, will you understand?

When I tell you that you will always be my baby, will you let me lie here and fall asleep next to you?

Let me share your dreams tonight?

What You Don't See

A wedding is a joyous occasion, full of love and laughter, but does the photographer see it this way?

I am your wedding photographer. I see it all.

Decadent guests arrive in clusters. Heads turn and take in the grounds, the décor. Women fawn over flowers and dresses. Children fight to break away from grownups' grips.

The deep hum of a cello hushes all chatter. Tuxedo-clad men line the stage, shifting and fidgeting. The groom watches the door and wrings his hands.

Music crescendos, and the audience stands. A confection of white appears, a spray of roses bloom at its center. Chiffon rustles as an angel glides toward a man. Dewy eyes are mesmerized by the ephemeral moment.

Hands join, and quivering voices recite their lines as vows are exchanged. Rings slide into place, lips meet, and cheers erupt. The violin joins the cello in celebration.

Guests rise and flow into the garden, into the heat of the day. Familiar faces find one another, outstretched arms embrace as kin welcomes kin.

Grandparents squeeze and pinch. Cousins, now grown, introduce girlfriends and boyfriends. Uncles shake hands. A new baby cries; an aunt coos. Estranged spouses exchange stiff smiles.

The sun burns bright. I adjust the exposure to capture practiced smiles. Sweat trickles and tickles my skin. I discern bloodlines, matching families, and lovers, and plus-ones to arrange the generations around the newlyweds. Arms loop through arms, hands on shoulders. I will freeze this moment.

Men straighten, women curve, suck in their stomachs. Fingers pick at spray-stiffened strands and smooth imaginary wrinkles, prolonging my shot. Smiles waver. Sweat gathers on foreheads.

Click. Click. Click.

I am your wedding photographer. I hear it all.

Family greets one another, always the same:

"You look great!"

"Let me see that baby!"

"Is this your lovely wife?"

"It's so good to see you."

"Your wedding next?"

I move through the crowd, invisible behind my lens. I collect truncated synopses of a dozen life events. Greetings begin with compliments and shared memories, end with career updates and personal accomplishments. I gather an uncle has made partner, a sickly aunt is now on the mend, a rascal bachelor has finally settled down–become a husband. The youngest of one family is all grown up, makes six figures. Another couldn't come; she just had a baby.

Some news is shared with breathless pride, some with shifting eyes and scuffling of shoes. A wayward son lives somewhere out West now. A married couple of seventeen years has separated, the kids aren't taking it well. Gray-haired relatives inquire about education. A young man explains he no longer wishes to be an engineer; he now works in retail. The subject shifts—what a hot day it is, everyone agrees.

Seated at the fringes, friends and acquaintances exchange, "how do you know the bride or groom?" in lieu of "hello." Location and occupation dominate the topic of conversation until commonalities build camaraderie. Chatter swells at the outskirt tables, laughter flows like champagne.

Click. Click. Click.

I am your wedding photographer. I know it all.

The bride drapes herself over her husband's arm, slurs a loud greeting to the nearest table. She teeters in her bedazzled stilettos. I attribute her discomposure to the Xanax she *borrowed* from a bridesmaid.

The coordinator is pleased that the ceremony went according to plan. I learned the latch on the dove cage had stuck right before the scheduled release, but a guest with a pocketknife came to the rescue. And the birds defecated on no one—another success.

I steal away with the wedding party for more photos. I pose and rearrange them like life-sized dolls. Dress shirts dampen under rented jackets, and mascara smears in the heat. Everyone is starving.

A bridesmaid giggles at a groomsman and bites her lip. He reciprocates with bedroom eyes, finding it hard to believe she is single. His last relationship ended a year ago, and the festivities amplify his loneliness. Tonight, he just wants to have a good time. I know she knows this too.

Returning to the reception, I find the caterers are relieved; a timer set in error nearly ruined the entrees. Disaster avoided, they remain on schedule and prepare to serve the guests. Waiters squirm under stress and heat, the kitchen more stifling than the humid summer air.

Guests mill about. Two women had worn the same dress, but they laugh and praise each other's style. They ask me for a picture.

Click. Click. Click.

I am the wedding photographer. I hear it all.

Lackluster "oh's" as dinner is served. The diminutive portions juxtapose with the grandeur of the event.

Knives clink against forks as gossip hovers over each plate of lukewarm chicken cordon bleu. Speculations circulate over who is to blame for the failed seventeen-year marriage or why an uncle not in attendance has declared bankruptcy. Clipped voices judge the decision to let Junior take over the family business.

One table over, jetlagged bridesmaids confide in one another, unanimously overwhelmed by the cost of being in the wedding. The honor of being included has no bearing on the price tag of airfare and silk dresses. They fan themselves in the heat.

The groom leads his wobbling bride toward a table of relics—bent, white-haired grandparents and great-grandparents who may never attend another wedding. He wants to introduce her to someone, but she whines—she needs a drink first. She pulls him away toward the sound of glass clinking against glass.

At the bar, a drunken groomsman flirts with a cousin. She mentions she's in high school and he chokes on whiskey.

Distant, silent, the groom's mother remains seated, watching her boy with his lively new bride. She barely speaks to the others. Her husband is skeptical. "She's a gold-digger. A fake," he hisses into his glass. He thinks his new daughter-in-law looks suspiciously well-endowed.

Someone announces it's time to cut the cake. Everyone crowds around the seven-tiered architectural masterpiece of sugar and flour. A bouquet of frosted flowers pours over the layers like a waterfall. I bend near the hands joined over a gold-plated knife as they slice into a cloud of buttercream.

Click. Click. Click.

I am your wedding photographer. I see it all.

The groom forks a dainty bite and poises it near his wife's lips. His smile is gleaming white against a summer tan.

She wavers, unsteady. Glassy-eyed with mischief in her smirk, she plucks a red icing rose from the top layer of the cake and mashes it into her new husband's teeth. He reels, shocked.

Napkin to mouth, he composes himself. He dabs a finger into white frosting and taps the tip of her nose—plays her game. The setting sun offers ideal light for capturing the challenge in her eyes.

She sinks her claws into the grandiose cake. Glossy French tips tinted scarlet, she grinds the glob into his waistcoat, dragging it down toward his belt-line.

And she laughs.

He stares, slack-jawed.

The guests suck in a collective breath.

A waiter intervenes, waving damp towels like white flags on a battlefield. The groom wipes his face and vest with gritted teeth.

Two groomsmen elbow each other in the ribs, hands over their mouths. A bridesmaid shakes her head and leaves.

A toddler standing to the side mimics the bride and thrusts a clammy hand into the base of the cake. His mother shrieks in horror, apologizing profusely.

Click. Click. Click.

I glance down at my screen and chuckle. *Got it.*

I am your wedding photographer, and I experience your wedding day in ways you never will. But when I send you the photos, you'll *ooh* and *ahh* and gasp at the crisp scenes, the soft light, and bright complexions. You'll be pleased with yourself for choosing such perfect colors and will be pleasantly shocked by how good you look. You'll point to guests in the background you forgot were there and will wish you'd had more time to talk to them. But it's alright, they look like they had a great time. You'll spend hours poring over each picture, trying to decide which one you should frame and hang over the fireplace.

What a magical day. Perfection.

When you see your pictures, you'll be blind to reality.

You won't recognize the gross display of vanity that was your *special day*. You won't remember the dysfunction. You won't see the exhaustion on your friends' faces, won't recognize disapproval. The concern, the uncertainty in the eyes of those older and wiser, will not register in your own. You won't see eyes reddened by alcohol. You won't perceive humiliation in the visage of a groom covered in wedding cake, disappointment in the droop of his lip.

You won't see the mortified face of a frazzled mother reaching for her pillow-cheeked toddler as he gazes in wonder at the monumental dessert stretching above him.

And you'll never know what a blazing hot, miserable scorcher your wedding day was.

Because *I* am your wedding photographer.

And I'm a damned good one.

At the Mercy of Your Choices

We cannot control everything or everyone–though some will try.

For the longest time, when I thought about who I was, I could only see you. When asked what I wanted, I would turn to ask you. Sometimes, I still do. I wouldn't be where I am without you, and for that, I am grateful, but those ties that once bound us have frayed and snapped and will never be what they were.

I was your obsession, even before I had a heartbeat. My existence was pre-plotted by you—you who consulted the calendar and mapped your cycles like stars in the sky, then aligned those nights for bodies to collide, and the seed of me took root within the shadowed depths of your womb. From that moment on, I was at the mercy of your choices.

When I was born, my little life was instantly set to the rhythm of the ticking of your internal clock. You were the sun, and everyone revolved around you. My days and nights played out according to your researched methods and schedules. You decided when I would eat, when I would be played with, and when I would rest before my needs and preferences could be voiced into language; I was helpless to do anything but accept your care.

And you *did* care. It was evident in the extraordinary lengths you took to regulate every facet of my life, all of which went unnoticed by me in those first few years. But

Dad was there through it all, a silent observer barred from uttering any word opposing your designs. I've heard him hiss—scattered, under-the-breath comments of the rigorous expectations you chained yourself to, how you set a series of timers to rule our days together, how you snapped at anyone who dared suggest you relax and relinquish the vision you had of your new life with me. But I was your first and your last, and you put your whole self into my upbringing.

When I was old enough, you chose a school for me—the best in the area—and we relocated to a district where tuition costs almost as much as our mortgage. I remember walking into that big empty house, where you'd already taped labels onto every door. *Master bedroom. Office. Jenna.* I lay on the floor of my new bedroom, watching the fan blades spin, and I dreamed of flying to a land where clocks didn't tick, and mothers didn't *tsk* at every misstep and mistake.

I remember you and me going to a department store together the week before school began. I had found a pair of pink sneakers covered with sequins, and I was enamored with the way they caught the light and glittered. *Fairy dust shoes* I called them. I clutched them to my chest and begged to have them, but you made me put them back, and I did. You had already filled a cart with items, and "shoes" had been checked off your list. You curated a new wardrobe for me, decided my whole *look*. I wouldn't be plain, but I wouldn't stand out. I needed to fit in here, you'd said, and make an impression as a good student.

And I was an impeccable student. I followed the rules, and you praised me for it. Teachers told you I was a joy in class, and that made you smile. I was bright and brimming with potential, and you proudly told the world I was your daughter. You laid expectations before me, and I never stopped reaching for them. When I was good, you loved me, and so I wanted to be the best.

As I grew older, I watched the children around me spread their wings and explore new territory. I tried to test the limits of my own nest, but my tether to you was short, and I couldn't even see over the edge. From day one, you told me what to wear, what to eat, when to rise, when to sleep. You told me who to be, and eventually the lines blurred between what you wanted and what I wanted.

But I never broke your rules, never bucked against your wishes. Mostly, because at the end of every day, I didn't have the energy to fight you. You filled every hour of my life with productivity, stimulation, and extracurricular activities. When you signed me up for dance classes, I squeezed into a leotard and practiced my stretches. When you drove me across town to take piano lessons with old Mrs. Weiss in her too-hot house, I brought my sheet music and my best manners. When you showed up at my school and signed me up for math competitions, I didn't release the steam that had been building. I kept my mouth shut, afraid I would explode.

Dad used to fight for me, used to stand up to you and insist you were putting too much on me. But he grew tired of losing, tired of being caught between the woman and the girl he loved, and tired of you turning that icy look on us both. When you were angry, the whole house felt cold, and so we tried to keep the peace.

When I grew taller and began to change the way young

girls do, you would watch me with a squint that stayed for every year my age ended in "teen". You'd walk by my room, peek your head in to check on me, then leave the door half open, as if I'd had demons, or drugs, or god-forbid a *boy* hiding in my closet. I would catch you looking over my shoulder at what I was reading and who I was messaging, always with a pinched look on your face as if nothing was good enough.

You didn't approve of any of my friends; they were bad influences—too brazen, too outspoken, and you did not want me to associate with them. And so I saw them at school, in those brief windows throughout the day when my time was my own and I could breathe air that hadn't already been exhaled by you. But when the bell rang and I walked down those stone steps, you were always waiting for me out front, where we'd drive home in silence to our mausoleum of dead dreams.

Family dinners became quiet affairs. You'd stare as I talked about my day at school—about new friends I'd made and where they were from—interrupting me to ask if "Taylor" was a boy or a girl. Dad would turn to you with that look of his own, the one where he shot one eyebrow up and cleared his throat, the look we both knew meant, "just leave her alone." You'd stop asking questions, and I'd stop talking altogether.

Over the summer, I wanted a job, but you set a stack of scholarship applications in front of me and said *that* was my job. You told me you and Dad would help with college, but only if I went to one of the schools on the three brochures in front of me. I was only a freshman then, but you wanted me to aim high and get an early start.

When my classmates began to drive, first in their parents' cars, then in vehicles of their own, I asked when I could get my license. You looked offended by my question, but simply said "not yet." That was your answer every time I asked, and so you continued to drive me to school. You liked those words: "no" and "not yet." I sometimes wondered if you even heard my requests before refusing them.

One ride to school turned into another and another until the day came when it would be my last ride. I cleaned out my locker and walked down those stone steps for the very last time. I donned a black cap and gown and delivered the valedictorian speech to my entire graduating class— something sweet and inspiring about spreading our wings— and then I was gone, and I didn't look back.

I would choose my own path. I didn't want your money, your stipulations. I didn't want your talons in me for one more minute.

My flight from the nest was not graceful. I crashed into trees and tore my face on sharp branches, and no one was there to pick me up and point out the way. I embraced every freedom that had been withheld from me, and my arms couldn't hold them all. I made mistakes, I took risks, I found out the hard way that not everyone is who they say they are, and not everyone wants to see you succeed. I learned how big the world is and how very small I am. I learned what it felt like to be used and deceived, lost and alone.

I questioned everything I thought I knew about myself, and I realized how angry I was with you–you who held me so closely that I couldn't breathe, couldn't see the world beyond the pictures of it you'd painted for me. I sometimes wondered if maybe you'd been held too tightly too, if suffocation was all you knew. But I stumbled through life, seeing things with new eyes, and eventually, I figured it out, and I made it to where I am today, all without *you*.

And then, I found love—a wonderful, resilient love, the kind of love that doesn't squeeze you so tightly it crushes you. The kind that embraces my *ugly* with my beauty, my failures with my successes—a love not dependent on constant perfection. It is real and raw and everything I never had.

We eloped on a Thursday and built a life together. And when I thought my joy was at its fullest, that love welled up and spilled over and created something pure and new—a seven -pound bundle of happiness we couldn't take our eyes off.

She is everything we could have hoped for, and nothing we could have prepared for. She tests our patience and makes us laugh all in the same breath. She's beautiful and messy and sweet and sour all at once. She's good and kind, strong and smart, and she has your eyes–eyes I haven't seen in a long time.

Her name is June. I want you to meet her, and I want you to love her for exactly who she is.

And I want her to know you because you're my mother, and I'll always love you.

Foretold In Smoke

A tale set within a fortune teller's parlor.

Marie S. 5/5 Stars

Vivienne is incredible! My life has completely changed since my visit. It's like a light came on and she's somehow unlocked all this hidden potential. She's the best, seriously just go. Call today!

Bradley J. 5/5

Worth every penny. Highly recommend.

Kevin R. 5/5 Stars

I never thought I'd come to a place like this, but when I was at an all-time low, I just needed someone to tell me if life was worth sticking around for. I wanted to know if it ever got better. Vivienne made me believe that it would. She told me true love was right in front of me, and now I'm dating my best friend and am the happiest I've ever been. She's the real deal.

Linda K. 5/5

Vivienne showed me the most beautiful future and now I am not afraid to go after my passions. Life changing.

I know your type. You're all the same. You come to me seeking something you believe life has withheld from you. Desperation hangs on you like a garment; you wear insecurity like a second skin. You shift and fidget in my doorway, hoping no one will recognize your car in the street and spread the word that you're seeking wisdom from a godless heathen and her crystal ball. Yet, here you are.

My polished greeting pulls you a few steps closer into the dimly lit room, where you stare at the artwork on the wall, trying to decipher its abstraction. You fumble over a compliment when I admit I painted it myself. Your nose twitches at the cloud of earthy smoke hanging in the stagnant air, and your ear tilts toward the sharp plucking of unfamiliar instruments—music trilling softly from a hidden speaker. The sound is heady, exotic, and raises the hair on your arms. The caricaturistic experience you expected is something different—it's alive, *sacred*, and it smells like singed aloeswood.

I sense the conflict within you—to stay or to flee, to grasp hold of your future and drag it into today, or to return to life as normal and submit to the natural process of discovery. You twist and wring your hands, afraid you're damning yourself or cursing your bloodline by setting foot in this den of witchcraft, or whatever it is they're calling it these days. But I am no one to fear; I am a respectable businesswoman. But you must make your own choice, so I remain silent, waiting for you to remember whatever it is that brought you here.

At last, you move. You approach me like I am an oasis in the desert, doubting what you see but desperately wanting it to be real. You are afraid to ask, afraid of the answers. I sense your struggle; I see your soft heart, your goodness and warmth, your suppressed potential suffocating under self-doubt. You are afraid to know what lies ahead because you have grown comfortable letting life rush by you. It is a river, coursing where it wills, and you are a leaf at its mercy. What

I tell you will alter the course of your life, not because the words on my lips drip with inherent power but because you will believe them.

You are the river. *You* are the force that cuts a path through the unknown, that courses where it wills. You are a rush of life, pure and sweet, with the power to shape and form and forge your own future.

My gift to you is no parlor trick, my predictions are not conjecture; I simply tell you what you are and what to look for, and you will find it every time.

I do not spin the threads of fate, but occasionally, I give them a gentle *pluck*.

***

Jim B. 1/5 Stars

Filing a police report. This woman is a scam artist.

Maurice W. 1/5 Stars

Waste of time and money. Basically told me my life was going to shit. Real downer. And the incense smelled like burnt hair.

Bryson D. 1/5 Stars

This is why I don't trust hippy-dippy, twinkle-dust, voo-doo garbage. Creepy art, obnoxious music, and some old hag just getting off on telling people how terrible their life is going to be. And no refund policy? Well, f*** you.

I know your type. You're all the same. You come to me seeking something you believe life has withheld from you. Arrogance hangs on you like a garment; you wear disdain like a second skin. You burst through my doorway, ignoring the closed sign in the window, insisting you just need a few minutes from this crazy lady and her crystal ball.

Your eyes adjust to the dimly lit room, and you squint at the artwork on the wall. You recoil, unsettled by its abstraction: its unorthodoxy disgusts you, makes you squirm. You cover your nose and cough against the cloud of bitter smoke hanging in the air, swishing your arms like an aggravated primate. The twanging of unfamiliar instruments rises above the silence, warbling from a hidden speaker. The sound is eerie, foreign, and makes gooseflesh ripple across your arms. The stock-image experience you anticipated is something altogether different—it's alive, *sinister*, and it smells like fire.

I sense no hesitation within you—you have come to grab the future by its horns and demand it bend and submit to your desires. You are impatient with life's natural process of discovery and want to know what obstacles lie ahead on the path on which you're blindly running. There is no fear of the consequences of knowing, no regard for how it will change the *now*. You want answers, and you will have them. You claim a chair and wait, twisting and wringing your hands impatiently until I join you across the small table.

You watch me like a stray dog you think might bite, your jaw set in defiance against anything you're prepared to reject. Because you don't want the truth. You want to be immersed in shimmering nonsense, to stretch out your palm and receive a shiny token of fabricated tales, to be placated by promises of a glowing future. I sense your coldness, your heart of stone, your resentment of everything that stands in your way. What I will tell you is the truth, and the truth will unfold as I tell it—not because I have cursed you, not because I am a she-devil hiding under beads and bangles, but because you are a curse to yourself. And you know it.

You are rot—an infection that will spread across all your days. Everything you touch will wither and die, and you can only blame yourself.

My words are not a hex on your soul, I don't speak out of malice; I simply show you what you already know.

I do not spin the threads of fate. I have no blade to sever their fibers.

But occasionally, I *test* the threads and hold a flame beneath the strands to watch and see what burns.

All for the Gold

A woman with questionable morals does what she must to survive in a rugged world of dust and gold diggers.

Hangtown, California. 1850.

Unrest is stirring in the camps. As soon as it was in the papers that there's gold in Coloma, men have been pouring into the area by the hundreds, and this town hardly seems big enough to hold them all. I've heard talk downstairs that if you stand in the middle of the tent camps, you can't even see where it begins or ends, that it's just a sea of sun-bleached canvas.

But I've never seen it myself, as I don't hardly leave this building. Madam Clancy says it isn't safe for us out there, that the men are gold-crazed and so long deprived of a woman, that they've become lawless—just grabbing women in the streets and having their way. At least in here, they pay for it, and good money too. By the time I'm done with this town, these diggers, I'm going to be rich. I'll go East and buy a house on the coast, with a big porch and blue hydrangeas. I had planned to leave last fall, but winter came swiftly and turned the roads to mush, and I was forced to wait until spring.

Madam says her and Mr. Clancy are taking care of my money till the day comes when I need it. They say it's not safe to keep your gold laying around—too many thieves in this town. But they don't know about my own private stash, my treasure pile in the back of my wardrobe. I've learned to be real good with my hands, and a drunk man in the arms of a prostitute isn't thinking about his pocket watch or the little bag of gold dust in his trousers. One nimble twitch of the fingers and he don't know what hit him.

The men slink out of my room, slipping into their suspenders like they've just come from the outhouse, while I lay there like a used handkerchief. My only consolation comes when I get up to add the stolen gold dust to my stash and watch the pile grow. Maybe I should feel guilty, knowing they might have had plans to send that hard-earned money back to their families, but why should I? They're the ones shelling out a fortune for women and whiskey; what's a little bit more? I know all too well the feeling of being taken from, and sometimes they need to be reminded how bad it hurts.

Every now and then the words of my mother, all proper like in her calico dress, come to mind. It's like I can hear her voice, high and quiet, saying, "remember what the Good Book says, Mary Anne; thou shalt not steal." I remember standing in the general store with Mama, I was maybe seven. She stood over me as I spilled my handful of salt taffy on the general store counter, crying, feeling like the whole world was watching. She made me fess up, give it all back. But she still bought me a piece anyway.

I haven't tasted taffy in years.

When I go East, maybe Baltimore, I'll eat so much taffy my insides will stick together. It's nearly spring and soon I'll be long gone.

***

It's been raining for days now, and the streets are so thick with mud they suck your boots right in. But rain's good for panning, so most of the men are down by the creek, praying and hoping for good luck, though the ones who find anything usually squander it all on a girl or else get robbed in the middle of the night. Last time it rained this hard, a fellow came in here with a hefty bag of dust, spent half on whiskey and Yuliana, then left, tripped off the boardwalk, and fell face-first in the mud. They found him the next morning, stiff and caked in red clay. Pockets empty, dust all gone.

Yuliana told me he'd wanted to marry her. Stupid girl. That's what they all say. Yuliana's new and still too excited about silk dresses and fresh milk to see the men as the rest of us do: sun-baked, delirious fools paying a month's earnings for half an hour with a public woman. And Madam charges more for her too, advertising that she has a *compliant disposition* and exotic beauty. And it seems the better Yuliana does, the worse the Clancy's treat me, and the less satisfied the men are. I used to be the favorite, the sweetheart. They'd touch my hair and tell me I was sent from heaven; now they go to her door, bringing flowers, and ribbons, and promising her the moon. Everyone always wants the shiny new toy.

The row of costumes in my wardrobe seem to mock me, their lace-trimmed bodices gaping open like they're wailing, wishing they could hug the curves of a more grateful patron like Yuliana. I shut the wardrobe doors, but it's like I can still hear them chiding, with a voice like my mother's. I remember walking through town together, past the dressmaker's shop, with its elegant displays in the window, and the milliners, with hats so beautiful I thought if I could own one, I'd never want for anything else. I'd press my face to the glass, and Mama would tug my arm, saying, "lovely, aren't they, Mary Anne? But never forget; thou shalt not covet."

It took her a year to save for a hat like the ones we saw in the window. A gift for my 10th birthday. The last gift she ever gave me.

I have no need to covet anymore; I wear the finest clothes a girl could desire. Yuliana will grow hardened and jaded like the rest of us; she'll learn to put on her makeup and put out a good show, and not let her heart get attached. She'll figure out how it really is, how everyone acts like they love you so long as you smile pretty and do what you're told.

When I leave this place, take the train across the hills and plains to a place where people will call me by whatever name *I* choose, I'll have my own life, and nobody is going to tell me what to do.

***

I can hear someone at the piano downstairs, playing something new and lively. I hear chips falling, glasses clinking, men laughing. I imagine Ivan, Clancy's right-hand man, scanning the room for trouble, which we rarely ever have. Ivan's easily the largest man I've ever seen in my life, with a head that goes nearly a foot above the doorway. He has a scar that runs from eyebrow to chin, pulling his eye into a permanent squint. And he's real quiet too. One of the girls says he's from a place where it's always winter, and frostbite probably got his tongue. Not much scares me anymore, but Ivan—he terrifies the living daylights out of me.

It's getting louder, and I know Clancy will want me to come down now, to lean over the tables of drunken gamblers, offering beer and bosom to thirsty eyes. I'll take my pick, the least filthy one at the table, and feed him sweet lies and empty flattery. "So you're the one all the girls are talking about," or, "I wonder if you're as good as you look." It makes them nicer, less heavy-handed. *Quicker.* The gambler swallows the liquid in his glass and hooks my waist with a dusty arm.

When we ascend the stairs together, I see Mr. Clancy nodding his approval from the card table, and Ivan staring from the bar. Madam Clancy waits at the top with a set of scales to weigh the man's dust, and a leather-bound notebook. Until we get more girls, Mr. Clancy says we have a *quota* to fulfill now, and Madam logs every exchange. They get real mean when we come up short.

Once, I snuck that damned book from Madam's room, planning to tear it to pieces and feed it to the woodstove, but she'd noticed it was missing almost immediately. So, I hid it in Yuliana's nightstand, then lied and told Madam I'd seen *her* take it. Yuliana might be the favorite, but that didn't stop Mr. Clancy from tanning her hide. I may hate her, but I didn't feel too good about that.

Yuliana's cries reminded me of the night Papa came home to us, drunk and all scraped up. We hadn't seen him for years, and everyone thought he was long dead. When Papa pushed his way in and saw the large boots by the door and the work coat on the hook, he banged, and cursed, and demanded to know if Mama'd been whoring around with another man. My mother was no whore, but she also was no liar. She told him the truth about her beau, and he nearly killed her for it. And when he'd gone and I had swept the glass off the floor and cleaned the cuts on her cheek, Mama whispered, mostly to herself, "Thou shalt not lie."

But here, in this godforsaken place, lying comes as natural as breathing.

***

My neck is painted with bruises, and my throat feels like sandpaper; I nearly died yesterday.

A wiry man from the camps had come in for a girl, wanting Yuliana in particular, but he didn't have enough gold and was mad as a hornet about it. He settled for me instead, but he made it clear that I wasn't the one he really wanted. He was all sharp angles and ruthless force, and I screamed when he clamped his dirty fingers onto my neck. That only made him squeeze tighter. Madam Clancy heard my cry and called for Ivan, who they said took the whole flight of stairs in three strides before rushing in and ripping the man off me. I heard later that the man couldn't walk when he was finally thrown out.

After the incident, I had made up my mind that I was done. Rain or shine, spring or not, I was leaving. I asked Madam Clancy for my money, deciding that I couldn't take one more day in this town. From my own records, I knew I should have had more than enough for a modest home out East and the train fare to get there, but when I asked for the total sum, she laughed in my face, a long, cackling sound. She told me I'd forgotten to account for room and board and a year's worth of luxuries like fine food, imported dresses, and perfume. She told me I still had months before my debts were paid.

If I hadn't been so weak, I would have killed her, right there. Dug my nails into her fleshy neck and choked the life out of her, just like that digger choked me. But they sent me away and told me to get rested up for work tomorrow. *Work.*

I didn't sleep a wink; I was too angry to sleep, too angry to cry. All I could do was think.

***

There's another hanging today. Apparently, a newcomer from Arkansas struck gold, ran his trap about it all throughout camp, then woke up to a couple of muckmen poking around his tent, looking for his stash. The newcomer started hollering and reached for his pickaxe, but the men shot him down, right there in his nightshirt. The thieves had been causing trouble for months, and the marshal thought it was time to make an example of criminals.

People here get real excited about hangings; everybody crowds the streets and acts like the circus has come to town. But I can't stand them. The last man I watched die at the end of a noose was my father. Though he never loved me, and all he ever did was cause pain for me and Mama, I didn't enjoy watching him die. Not like that.

It's nearly sundown, and the saloon is empty—a rare sight. No one sits at the bar, the card tables are deserted, and the other girls are hanging off the front porch watching the thieves being walked up onto the rickety platform. My stomach is lurching, not because of the hanging, but because I'm leaving. Right now. With only a day dress and my sack of stolen dust and trinkets, I fly down the stairs and turn down the shadowed hallway, ready to walk out the door and never look back. I just have to make a little visit to Mr. Clancy's office first.

The heavy door creaks like it's trying to betray me. I should have known that even the hinges in this establishment would be loyal to the Clancy's. The air in the windowless room is stagnant, and warm, and smells like cigar smoke. When my eyes adjust to the dim light, I locate the black vault in the corner and quickly realize I've misjudged my abilities as a thief. I twist the dial at random and yank the handle as panic rises in the pit of my stomach. There must be a combination somewhere, I think. Maybe in the desk.

I try every drawer, rummaging through stamps, and steel nibbed pens, and bits of paper, and merchant receipts, but none that appear to have a vault combination written on them. One thin drawer at the desk's center is locked, but I don't have the key. I shake, and pull, and rip at the drawer before falling in a heap on the floor. *Blast it all.* What a fool I am to have thought I could ever leave this place, a stupid girl for letting myself hope.

A shadow falls over the desk, and I lift my face slowly. I can feel my heartbeat in every tender bruise, like it already knows another blow is coming.

Towering over me, over the desk, and filling the entire room is Ivan, standing with arms crossed over a rippling chest. He takes in my plain clothes and my canvas sack, and I know there's nothing I can say. All I can do is hang my head and wait for the pain.

The shadow moves and pauses by the vault, where a series of mechanical clicks fills the silence. He pulls the handle and the door swings open, its iron wall as thick as a man's arm. In a flash, he shuts the door and returns to where I'm cowering under the desk. He bends and places a bag of gold in my hand—and not just gold dust, but I can feel whole nuggets bulging against the pouch. "Ivan?"

He helps me up and pushes me out of the office and toward the back door. "Ivan, why are you helping me? Clancy's going to kill you for this." At that, he huffs–a quick, voiceless burst of air.

We spill onto the back steps and hear the whoops and cheers of the crowd in the town's square. Someone's been hung. Crickets chirp as the last light dips below the horizon.

"Why, Ivan?" I try again.

His voice is deep, accent sharp and strange—nothing like the slow drawls of folks around here. "The laborer is werthy of 'is wages."

And with that, he lets the screen door close and returns to the saloon.

I stand there for a moment, dumbfounded until I hear another round of cheers from the street. The second man is dead.

And then I run. And I don't look back.

Dust in the Cornbread

Drought, dust, and the Great Depression take more than they give from a Mid-Western American family.

There's dust in the cornbread. I can hear the grit as the girls chew beside me. Beige flecks float in their cups of milk.

"Where's papa?" the youngest asks.

"Don't talk with your mouth full."

"But, Mama—"

"Please just eat."

The seat at the head of the table remains empty even after we've finished our food. I pump a stream of water into the sink and set the dishes inside. "I'll be back."

The late afternoon sun is blinding. I find him standing in the middle of the rows of withered corn stalks, their leaves curled and brown. They never made it past the tops of our boots. The sickening scene stretches across all 300 acres, dead stumps dancing in the heat.

"Come in and eat something. I made—"

"We're gonna lose the farm." His voice is a raspy, choking sound. His brown hair lifts in the breeze and curls around his dirty collar.

"We're gonna make it," I whisper to his back, my lips as dry and cracked as the land. "It's gonna be alright."

He kneels and rips a plant from the dry, packed earth and hurls it into the sky. Then one more, then another until he's cleared a whole row. He pounds his fists into the barren soil; sweat soaks his shirt. My tears fall on the flour-sack dress stretched across my swollen stomach, then almost instantly evaporate in the heat. The babe kicks, as if he too felt the weight of those tiny drops.

***

The windows rattle, and the door shakes, threatening to burst open and welcome in the wrath of the whipping, black winds.

"Mama—"

"Don't talk. Try not to breathe it in."

The wet towels draped over the kitchen table do little to keep the fine dust of a thousand acres of Kansas topsoil from finding its way into our eyes, our teeth, our lungs. The oldest holds her sister, who hacks and cries, their faces mottled with dirt and tears. I clutch the baby against my chest, but he thrashes and wails in protest. His cries are drowned out by the storm; it's like a train is tearing through the walls.

It's nearly night when the roar of the wind dies down, and the house is still. We'd fallen asleep in a tangle of limbs, heads resting against shoulders. My dress is stiff with dried sweat, and my joints crack when I extend my legs. The baby sleeps.

Like freshly fallen snow, a powdery layer of dust coats the counters, the floors, the furniture. We moisten rags and wipe the crusted grime from our eyes. One of the girls gets the broom. The other follows me to the bedrooms. We strip the sheets from each mattress and shake them until they resemble something akin to white again.

The door opens, and a wind-blown man with the stature of my husband stumbles inside, face coated with a thick layer of dirt—unrecognizable.

"You get caught in it again?"

"I was out with the cows." He hangs his hat on a hook. "Couldn't get them to come back to the barn."

"But did you?" I search his face. "Did you get them inside?"

He collapses in a kitchen chair and lets his head fall into his hands. "Only one."

**

Henry's first birthday falls on a hot, arid Tuesday. We sell eggs in town and buy sugar with the money. His cake is simple but sweet; we eat every last crumb. His father presents him with an opened-mouthed fish carved out of a hunk of broken fence post. Henry gnaws it with his two front teeth.

"Son," he scoops Henry up and sets him on his knee. "When you're older and the rains come back, I'll stock the pond with bass and brim–teach you to catch a real fish." Henry cranes his neck back and grabs a fistful of his father's beard. Then he coughs.

**

"Another chicken died, Mama."

"Great."

"Where should I put her?"

"With the others, I reckon."

"I'll get the shovel."

***

The mattress squeaks. He tosses and turns next to me. In the light of the moon, I see his face pointed up toward the ceiling, eyelids blinking in the darkness, and I know he's thinking about rain. I place a hand on his chest, let it slide to his hip—offer myself for comfort, for distraction, but he turns away, his back a wall between us.

He used to reach for me, find my hands, my lips in the middle of the night when sleep wouldn't come. When the rains first stopped and the dust storms came and took everything from us, we still gave of each other. When the dust blocked the sun and choked out the crops, we still found life in each other's arms. When our bellies went hungry so the children could eat, our hearts stayed full, and hope mollified the dull pangs.

But hope ran out a long time ago, and there's nothing left to fill the empty spaces.

***

There are no more flowers, so I tear a strip of cotton from my apron and tie it in a neat bow. It sags in a pitiful heap beneath the plank jutting out of the earth–and the name etched across its wooden face.

Henry: 1934-1935

My husband lies prostrate beside it, sprawled in the dirt, talking to the sun-bleached board. I lower myself beside him and rest my hand on his head, his brown hair now showing streaks of gray. But he doesn't even look at me, just continues to mutter to the grave as if I wasn't there. He says something about Henry "having sway way up there," and maybe he could "ask about rain."

Henry was born in a dust storm, gasping for that first breath, and Henry died in a dust storm. His little lungs never knew clean air. Back when the fields were green and my husband stood tall in the midst of them, I labored over gowns and booties, knitted blankets for each new child growing inside me. But I made nothing for Henry; somehow, I knew then that the world he'd be brought into would not be kind to him. I sometimes wonder if there was dust in the womb.

***

We stare at the door, spoons poised over our stew. The knock comes again.

"Honey?"

His chair scrapes against the floor, and he goes to the door, then slips out onto the porch. Through the window, I see a man in a brown suit, briefcase in one hand. His face is pinched and sunburned. They don't talk for long.

When my husband comes back inside, he crumples a sheet of paper and throws it against the wall. Then he strides to the bedroom and slams the door.

"Mama?" The oldest turns to me. "What's wrong with Daddy?"

I watch the cloud of dust following the man's automobile as he drives away—a black speck in an endless expanse of brown.

"Come on, let's get these dishes cleaned up."

The girls stand and carry their bowls to the sink. I retrieve the balled-up paper and smooth it against my lap. The bolded word *foreclosure* jumps from the page and takes up residence in the hollow pit of my stomach.

***

He isn't beside me when I wake up. He doesn't meet me in the kitchen for coffee or join us at the table for lunch. I don't see him standing in the fields, and the barn is empty but for one emaciated cow. We eat dinner without him, then draw and heat water for the bath.

"You girls go ahead. I'll be right back." The screen door slams behind me, stirring up a puff of dust around the doorframe.

Clouds move like paint in the lavender sky, warm yellows and oranges swirling with the cool shades of evening. It's almost beautiful enough to make me forget the barren wasteland below. But not quite.

I find him behind the barn, straddling an overturned bucket. He sits before a crater of dirt and debris, humming a jaunty tune. He holds a fishing pole in his hands. He winds the reel, checks his hook, then casts the line back into the pit. The hook catches on a scrap of metal poking out of a heap of dust. He tugs it free, reels in his line, and recasts, sending it further into the sunken pit of windblown earth. His shoulder is skin and bone under my hand.

"The girls are wondering where you are. They're worried about you." I choke out a whisper. "*I'm* worried about you."

He winds his reel again, then inspects his hook and laughs. "Forgot my bait."

"Honey. Please."

His hair looks nearly all brown again in the warm light of the sunset. He turns the reel and curses when the hook returns empty.

"Fish just ain't biting today. Maybe I'll have better luck on the other side."

The cow bellows from the barn; its hungry cries are a knife to my insides. I tug the pole from his hands and kneel before him, skirts draping over his dusty boots. His stubbled cheeks snag against my rough, dry palms.

"We're going to get through this. I need you to believe that."

I bring his head level with mine, but he looks through me—past me at the miles and miles of bleakness.

"Did you hear that?" he whispers.

"Hear what?"

"Thunder."

A drop hits my cheek.

Then another.

Once, I Was Magnificent

Everything deteriorates as the years go by, but love will not be worn down by time.

I turn 100 years old today, though there isn't much left of me worth celebrating. I am only a fragment of what I used to be—a pitiful, yellowed artifact from days long gone. I have no purpose, no beauty left to contribute to this world.

But once, I was magnificent.

***

100 years ago, before I was stitched together with such tedious attention, I was of a more disconnected nature— rather, I was not yet myself. Before my inception, I was a bolt of satin, a pouch of pearls, a spool of white thread perched on a shelf, waiting to be selected for a creation that would transform a peasant into a princess.

I was only strips and disconnected pieces when that doe-eyed lover first conceived of me, first pointed at each part and chose it for her masterpiece. I was trimmed and measured and cut from the mother cloth, then wrapped in brown paper and carried out into the world. She brought me home and made me who I was.

Her hands were gentle yet deft, and she worked with the fervor of one stricken with lovesickness. Her foot guided the pedal, which turned the wheel, which moved the needle— the needle that pierced every part of me and fashioned me into a work of art. I was a confection of lace, ruffles, and layers, and the length of me dragged the floor when my maker stepped into me and sauntered around the room.

She gazed in the mirror, at us together, and glowed. She turned and twirled, inspecting every inch of me—each seam, each bead, each panel of satin—then she slipped out of me with the utmost care and returned me to my silk-lined hanger. I hung there as she counted down the days until we'd walk down the aisle together, when the whole world would see how I swished against her long legs, how I hugged her wrists in such an elegant taper, how the dozens of silk-covered buttons along my back side trailed down her spine in a most becoming arc.

I don't deny that I was beautiful—not out of haughtiness or to put other garments to shame, but in due honor of my maker's brilliant craftsmanship, her hours of laboring over each measurement, snip, or minute stitch. Being torn from the mother cloth had left a sort of aching within me, and I was apprehensive of what I would become, but when that day arrived, when I was completed, she took me in her arms and wrapped herself in my white flesh, and we departed as one.

Our debut was glorious. We were an irresistible force of grace and beauty. My maker's beloved couldn't take his eyes from us. He had gaped at us as we first walked toward him, and he continued to stare at us the whole evening, always touching our arm with his calloused fingers. His presence was suffocating, how closely he pressed against my seams, even stepping on my hem with his boxy, leather clad feet. In his heady infatuation with my maker, he let crumbs of yellow cake trickle down and settle into the fabric at our throat, icing smearing into Chantilly lace.

But his carelessness could not damper our beauty. Everyone was enamored with us. No one passed without eyeing the picture we made together, her body in mine. People reached for us, to feel the smoothness, the fullness of our sleeves, or to squint at the meticulous detail of our beaded neckline.

We were royalty—an image of heavenly divined authority. A crown on our head would have completed us, but crown or not, we looked fit to rule.

The night came to an end, that glorious night, when a shiny black carriage decked out in streamers pulled up to the stairs and we rushed toward it—my maker and I, and her lover—her husband. People cheered and tossed fistfuls of rice in the air. It fell in her hair and down into my ruffles. Inside the carriage, he scooted close and crowded us, sitting on my skirt and crushing me with his hips. He distracted her with his attention, and she did not heed my predicament.

When we arrived home, suitcases waited by the door, all clasped and stacked in a neat pile, his with hers, a hatbox on top. I wondered which suitcase they would put me in.

Moonlight shone through the window when my maker lifted her arms above her and began to undo my buttons. She fumbled and struggled, the silk domes slipping in her shaking hands, and he stepped in to assist. His hands were clumsy and thick and too hasty, not gentle like hers. My little fabric loops felt stretched, my delicate stitches stressed.

A rush of cool air filled my form when she stepped out

of me and draped me over a chair, where I lay through the dark night. Strange sounds filled the room, and shadows danced on the ceilings, but I was left over the chair—an afterthought. When the sunlight returned, my maker came to me and held me to her and touched me softly. Then she placed me on a hanger and hung me in a dark closet.

The house grew cool and drafty, the air stale. Everything was quiet; I was alone.

How could she have just peeled me off and cast me aside? After the countless hours she had poured into me, was this the end?

I remained there until I lost count of the days, accepting that my life had run its course when suddenly the closet door opened, and a rush of air poured in. My maker stood in the afternoon light, a vision of health and happiness. She took me up in a final embrace before I was folded upon myself and laid in a dark, wooden box where her face became a sliver and then disappeared entirely as she lowered the lid over me.

***

Sunlight pierced my quiet resting place, the place where I had given up counting the days, which quickly had turned into years. I'd resigned myself to an eternity in that cedar coffin when the light flooded in, and a young woman's face appeared above me. She leaned over and lifted me from the chest. Creases lined my bodice, my arms; my folds fell open as I was held.

Her hands pulled at me and opened me up, and her unfamiliar body filled my empty spaces. Her shoulders were narrow, her ribcage wide. Her arms were too short, and her neck too long. It was all wrong, the body inside me. Nothing was as I remembered; this could not be my maker.

Her eyes in the mirror were new and bright, but buried in their swirling depths lay something familiar. Who was this imposter? This short-haired girl with wavy curls and rouged cheeks?

There were others beside us. They pinched and pinned and turned us this way and that way. Finally, the girl removed herself from me, and I was laid upon a table.

Snip. Snip.

What were they doing to me? Somewhere I was being cut, the stitches at my shoulder pulled and undone—pressure on all sides, tingling as threads slipped from their lines. They held up my sleeves, now disconnected and flat, and took them away.

This mutilation continued, and I lay helpless.

When it ended, I was hung on a wooden hanger where they ogled and fondled me with a sort of intoxicated infatuation.

Then, that pink-cheeked girl took me down and clothed herself in what remained of me. She paraded around the room, my skirts flapping against her ankles. I no longer trailed along the floor. She strode over to the mirror and stopped, her lips parting in a gleaming smile. She brushed her hands softly along my sides, fingering my beads ever so gently.

I almost didn't recognize myself. Gone were my full

sleeves with their tapered cuffs and gone was my train that followed me like a loyal guard. I was sleek and exciting, with a dazzling burst of beads along my chest.

Together, we glowed.

And standing behind us, hands on our shoulders—those hands I could recognize by the faintest caress—stood my maker, her proud gaze christening me on the day of my rebirth. Those faces in the mirror were so alike, the same eyes bright with joy.

Soon, I was debuted to the world yet again, in my appended, modern form. I was wiser this time and understood the temporality of the pomp and laud associated with the occasion. Another lover with leather-clad feet attached himself to us for the entirety of the day and into the night, but it did not vex me so much this time. It was clearer to me now that he was the reason I had been brought out of purgatory and revived, and for that, I owed him my gratitude.

Once again, when the festivities were over, I was carefully detached from my wearer and draped over a dresser mirror. The evening carried on much like the one I remember from years before, but this time I knew to anticipate the long night that would soon befall me.

Before the month's end, I was cleaned and wrapped in tissue paper and laid to rest in a cedar chest where my layers settled and compressed for an eternity of darkness.

***

Beads clattered to the floor when someone lifted me from my resting place. A girl with bright red lips and dark, coiled hair piled at her temples pulled me from the chest and held me against herself, smiling. My bodice sagged, and there was a tear at my waist, but she smiled, nevertheless. She placed me in a bag and brought me to a shop where women bent over whirring machines, chattering, cutting, and pinning.

I was laid out flat and scissored down to strips—my skirt in halves, my bodice flayed open on a hard table. They picked over me, selecting some pieces and discarding others. The hum of the machine filled the room as its needle moved in a flash, and I was adjoined to new fabrics—thicker and more vibrantly white: I was becoming a fresh creation.

When the piercing and poking was done, and my new wearer was satisfied, she took me in her arms and stepped into me, and we stood together in a room of mirrors. My skirt fell longer and graced the top of the floor. I had sleeves once again—simple and tasteful with silk-covered buttons at the cuffs. My beads and pearls had been painstakingly resewn along my neckline, and the beautiful lace that had once hugged my first maker's delicate throat was now attached to a sweeping veil that trailed behind us like angel's wings.

And together, we glowed.

Soon we would capture the eyes of everyone in the room and steal the breath of a man at the end of an altar. He would run his hands along our arms and tell us how marvelous we looked. I would not scoff at his touch, for I would know it came from a place of love—a love that will bring more joy and happiness to my wearer than I ever could. And I would not begrudge him that.

But that day never came; there was no fairy tale.

It was an Autumn day that passed like any other. The sun rose as it always did, but the dark-haired girl did not step out to greet it. She laid in her bed, staring in silence at the grid of shadows the sun cast on the wall. When the light grew golden and dim, she peeled herself away from her bed and came to me. She stepped into me with trembling legs and left me unbuttoned, her back exposed to the drafty room, and she sat alone in a heap on the floor, tangled in her lace veil. Her curls fell in limp waves, and red lipstick stained our sleeves. Tears slid down her cheeks and fell on to the thick, folded triangle of red, white, and blue fabric she clutched in her hands. She touched the white stars embroidered on a sea of blue, and she wept. On the dresser, a framed photograph of a young man with cropped hair and kind eyes gazed down upon us, pride visible in the tilt of his square jaw.

I could only hug her weary shoulders as they shook.

We shook together.

***

I don't remember how long I laid in a heap on that floor or on a hanger in the closet, but in time, I was swept up and stowed away and carried up above the house where the air was perpetually stagnant and hot. Time slipped by like a bolt of silk unraveling and twisting into one great, shimmering pile. Years ran together. Sound did not reach my resting place, light did not pierce its walls. I laid with one lipstick-stained arm folded over the other, alone with the memories of my wearers to keep me company, and I rested.

Time is a curious thing. Stones sleep through centuries

as trees stand watch, oceans shift and steal away islands, and mountains yawn as one millennium ends and another begins, but fabric is no match for time. The air discolors it, moths eat away at it, and the years simply wear it down.

I have seen 100 years and can attest to this. I am yellowed and moth-eaten, wrinkled and tattered, but I have had a full life, a wonderful life. I knew my usefulness would be short-lived, temporal—but the love that was stitched into me, the love that filled me and carried me into another's arms over and over, is not worn away by time—not even by death.

I was once magnificent, and I always will be.

Letters to the Sun

A woman writes to her lover, hoping to heal an old rift, but is it too late?

December 3, 1944

Dear Roger,

I must be the last person on earth you'd ever thought you'd receive a letter from, but I hope you can overcome the shock of it to read what I have to say.

I am deeply ashamed that it has taken all of two years to muster up the courage required to put pen to paper and post this letter. I pray the mere act of unfolding these pages does not reopen old wounds. And if you cast these papers in a puddle and stomp them underfoot, I would understand. I would probably do the same.

I will be brief; I miss you Roger, and I was a fool, a blind fool.

There is no way to measure the loss. In my rash and thoughtless unfaithfulness, I not only lost the love of a good man, but I lost a friend—a friend whose absence casts a gray pallor where there was once vibrance, whose strength lent assurance to everyone around him.

You were gold, solid and pure, and I was wrong, plain and simple.

Forgiveness is a gift I do not deserve, and I expect you

must be angry. I know I hurt you. All I can hope for is that you'll accept these painfully belated words as the truth—the truth as sincere as it could be.

Humbly yours,

Alice

***

January 17, 1945

Dear Roger,

I am still in disbelief at my own audacity. You must be furious. To be betrayed, then abandoned, then forgotten, only to have me wriggle my way back into your life like a pestilence; I did betray you, and there is nothing I can say to remove that stain, that blight. I was brash and careless—a child, captivated by something shiny and new, but I have never forgotten you, not for one moment.

I was *nothing* to him, and he is nothing to me.

He vanished from my life much in the same way he came: suddenly and arrogantly, looking ahead only far enough to discover the next thrill. He was a bolt of lightning that struck the black sky in a dazzling display of electricity, and just as quickly, he dissipated into a wisp of smoke.

But *you*. My dear, dear Roger, you are the *sun*. You burn bright and strong, faithfully lighting the sky each and every morning without fail. And much like the sun, I took your warmth for granted. Now, everything is hard and cold. It all feels so lifeless without you.

My greatest regret is not seeing what was right in front of me. You are farther away from me now than you've ever been. Oceans stretch between us, time warps from my day to yours, but I see it more clearly now than I ever did.

You were a treasure, and I was a fool.

It is preposterous of me to consider you will even respond to my letters. So much time has passed, I wonder if the rift is too wide to cross. You have likely moved on, found happiness with someone new. If so, I pray she values you the way I should have, and I wish every happiness on your life.

Only yours,

Alice

**

March 13, 1945

Roger,

I am so sorry. For all of it.

Sincerely yours,

Alice

**

April 25, 1945

Roger,

With this final letter, you will be free of me. I will say my piece, then sever all ties between us and consider no longer the sliver of a chance that you might forgive me and that we could return to what we once were.

I am deeply sorry for the pain I caused you, the pain you folded into your bag and slung over your shoulder and carried with you into a sea of uniforms. I hated myself for letting you walk away without trying to make things right. I was too stubborn, too proud to admit what I am finally able to say today: none of it was worth it. Not for a second.

Enclosed in this envelope, you'll find the ring you placed on my finger on the night of our engagement. I will never be free of the guilt I carry for tainting the significance of such a gift, for dragging your faithfulness through the mud, still I will always be thankful for the light you brought into my life. Your friendship was worth the world to me. Your love filled every crack and hollow and made me believe that anything was possible.

I would cross this ocean to turn back time and undo the damage I've done, but in my stead, I send these words, your ring, and all my love.

Forever yours,

Alice

***

May 25, 1945

Alice,

It seems your letters have been on quite a journey. They must have followed our battalion halfway across Europe and finally caught up with us now that the war has come to an end. But when they finally landed in my hands, I will say, it was a bit of a shock.

I have heard nothing from you for almost two years, and now here I am with a stack of wrinkled, inked-up envelopes, covered in your looping scrawl. I hardly know where to start, Alice.

But let me put you at ease with this: I forgave you a long time ago. And though I am empty, I am not angry. You may have hurt me, but I hold no grudge, and it pains me to think you've carried the weight of such assumptions for so long. So, please consider this permission to let that weight go.

Your admission has cleared some of my misunderstandings, and for that, I thank you. The uncertainty of it all has been a wound that wouldn't seem to heal. In the bitterest of winter nights and in the sweltering heat of day, I've been racking my brain to understand why—what it was about me that pushed you into the arms of another.

You're dynamite, Alice. You shook my world like no one else ever has, and you made me see life in a whole new way. You are a rainbow in all of this fog.

I know I'm a simple man. I'm a quiet fellow, a terrible dancer, and I might not excite you the way he did, but I've never stopped loving you. Not for one moment.

In my deepest exhaustion, I've loved you. In my fevered dreams, I've loved you. In the chaos of battle and in the face of death, I have loved you. And now that this war is over— OVER! Alice, it's over—I am coming *home*. And when I do, I've got a little gold ring burning a hole in my pocket that belongs to a beautiful girl in Oklahoma.

Still yours,

Roger

William Raymond Lawson, Is that You?

A man returns to his hometown. Will he find the closure he is looking for?

Old Mr. Bill was long gone from this world when a neighbor finally found him, slumped in his chair with a cat curled at his feet. The poor woman didn't expect to find him dead, though at his age, no one should've assumed he'd live much longer, but the shock of his death was nearly overshadowed by what she found in his home: an overwhelming and astonishing volume of artwork. Paintings hung on almost every square inch of the walls, some on simple canvases, others in gilded frames. They lined both sides of the hallway and the stairwell leading up to the second floor. There were even stacks of unhung paintings propped against a sofa.

Most were landscapes, scenes in sky blues and forest greens that seemed to bring the outdoors in, with one location recurring as the subject of dozens of paintings—a waterfall trickling into a river. The falls were narrow and somewhat hidden beneath an overgrowth of trees, no grandiose world wonder, but the artist made it look like an Eden. With masterful strokes, they had painted light rays cutting through the foliage to kiss the streams of water. Glistening white beads of spray rose out of the mist, like a celestial being ascending from within the falls.

Each painting was uniquely beautiful, but in the corner of every one were the same, unmistakable looping initials signed in blood red paint.

**

Gravel crunches under my tires as I weave higher up the mountain. The thing about mountain towns is that the deeper in you go, the more it seems like Time himself got turned around and couldn't find his way along the winding dirt roads.

When I had driven through town, it looked a bit fresher than I remember, with new signs on storefronts and freshly paved sidewalks, but the farms and cabins along the route to my family's property look nearly the same as they did five years ago. Besides seeing the occasional tractor in place of a horse-pulled plow, not much has changed.

My Ford bumps over dips and holes in the gravel road like it's not sure if it was made for this kind of terrain. I pass the Martin's place and wave to Mrs. Martin hanging her laundry on the clotheslines, but she only stares, understandably. She wouldn't recognize my car.

And probably doesn't recognize me either.

For the hundredth time since pulling out onto the highway with a crisp map in the passenger's seat, my stomach rolls and I wonder if I'm making a huge mistake.

The hill is getting steeper as I get closer, and my knuckles are stiff over the steering wheel. I recognize the Schulz's property around the next bend, where a rusty mailbox hangs open at the road. My palms grow moist, my breathing uneven. I hurry on. I work the gas pedal lower, gaining momentum for the next steep curve, and nearly fly right past the driveway to the house. Branches hit my window as I roll in.

I leave the key in the ignition and squint through the bugged-up windshield; the house is nothing like the images from my memories. Its paint is faded, the flowerbeds are overgrown and scraggly with weeds, and moss grows along the shaded part of the house—like the entire structure is becoming part of the mountain. The old oak tree we used to play under as kids stands as strong as ever, as if five years was just a short nap. Its branches are thick with vibrant summer growth, and a rope dangles in the breeze where a tire swing once hung.

Cows graze on the edge of the hill and down in the sunlit valley where a figure walks among them with a subtle limp—his souvenir from the first war.

Papa.

My stomach rolls again, and I consider backing out and driving away before anyone knows I've come, but before I can make up my mind, the front door opens, and someone steps onto the porch.

Mama.

Pinpricks of guilt sting my eyes. She's aged much in the same way the house has, her skin faded and tired, and I can't help but feel that I've caused it. I step out of the car and remove my hat. She shuffles down the porch steps, shielding the sun from her eyes with a wrinkled hand, and then she stops.

Her mouth hangs open. "William Raymond Lawson, is

that you?"

I clutch my hat to my chest, not sure what to do with my hands. "Yes, Mama, it's me. I'm sorry, I should have written first."

She stands there for a moment, staring, and I wonder if she's heard me. Her face is void of all expression, and my deepest fear bubbles to the surface; *they haven't forgiven me. I shouldn't have come.*

And then she takes a step, and another, and then throws her wiry arms around me. She is so small now, so fragile in my arms, and I'm afraid to break her, but I don't want to let go.

She pulls away and holds my head in between both hands. "Your hair's so short." She chokes out the words.

I run a hand across my scalp, "I had to cut it back when I joined up."

"You enlisted?" Her lip quivers.

"As soon as I left."

"I don't understand; how? You were just a boy." Her voice trailed off.

"I was tall. They didn't ask too many questions."

She blinks back tears. "You look just like your father did."

My insides twist. "Papa—how is he? Is he still angry?"

Her face falls, and she looks away. "Your Papa. He took it hard, Will, harder than any of us. I won't lie to you." She kicks at a rock in the driveway. "Things were so difficult–with your sister, with the farm. He felt like you just abandoned us when we needed you most."

A wave of shame washes over me, and my stomach rolls like I'm caught in a tempest. I feel sick, and all I want to do is run, run away like I did all those years ago.

"You know I couldn't stay, Mama. Every single day I had to look at her and see her pain and know there was nothing I could do to make it go away—it was *torture*."

"I know," Mama says.

"I just didn't know what else to do, but I couldn't stay."

She nods her head, not looking at me.

"I told myself when the war was over—if I made it through—I was going to come back here, come and make things right."

Mama squeezes my hand and smiles, lips tight.

"Mama, what about Elsie? How is—is she—"

Her voice is soft. "Would you like to come in and say hello?"

***

They say you don't appreciate what you have until it's gone. Growing up here, I was surrounded by beauty, and until I left home, I never knew how different life could be, how in big cities, people lived stacked on top of one another like building blocks with barely a window to let in the sunlight—a patch of communal grass for a backyard.

For us—Elsie and me—the *world* was our backyard. We'd come home after school, kick our shoes off on the porch, and disappear. Papa would call from the barn, "just look after your sister, Will," as we took off into the woods. In the summer, we'd spend nearly every day at the river, sunbathing like turtles on big rocks or fishing from the riverbank with chunks of spam on our hooks. And if you followed the river upstream, about a mile's hike from our property, there was a beautiful waterfall we claimed as our own.

When it rained, Elsie and I would hide behind the falls and pretend we were survivors from a shipwreck, waiting for someone to rescue us. When the river was shallow, we'd look for fossils along the bank and pretend we were archeologists at a secret dig site.

Elsie and I were always close when we were little. We did most everything together and didn't see a problem with it—until the summer the Schulz family moved to the area. They had three boys around my age, and we became fast friends—inseparable, especially as we got older. We'd trap crawdads in the river or hike to the top of the falls in our matching coon skin hats, where we'd hang hammocks in the trees. We believed we owned the mountain, and on our mountain, there was no room for little sisters.

The day Elsie followed us up the river was the day the Schulz boys and I had just finished building a tree fort at the top of the falls. We were sitting across the wooden slats with our legs over the edge, hunting squirrels with slingshots, when we saw Elsie coming up the hill, holding her favorite kitten in her arms like a baby.

"Will, look." The oldest boy pointed, "we've got a trespasser."

"Yeah," said the middle boy, "a girl!"

I played along. "And she's bringing that flea-ridden cat! She'll heap a curse on our whole camp!"

Then we spat like cowboys.

Elsie reached the top, and we climbed down from our fort, holding nubby sticks in our mouths like cigars.

"What do you want, Elsie?" I said.

"Can I play with you?" she asked, leaning over to catch her breath.

"No girls allowed," said the youngest Schulz boy.

"Yeah. Isn't that right, Will?" said the oldest.

"That's right." I crossed my arms. "No girls allowed."

"Please," she whined. "I'll play whatever game you guys want."

The oldest Schulz boy threw a meaty arm around my shoulder, his voice low. "Let's play, *steal the cat.*"

I nodded in agreement, and we broke apart and dove toward Elsie. I pulled at her wrists while the other boys tried to wrestle the cat from her.

"No!" She squealed, squeezing it tighter. I finally managed to peel her fingers away from the cat's torso, and it dropped to the ground, hissing. One of the boys lunged forward, chasing it with flailing arms. The kitten inched backwards, baring its pointy teeth, and then suddenly disappeared over the edge of the falls.

"No! No!" Elsie shrieked, breaking out of my grip and running to the spot where it fell.

We all stood like statues, eventually inching our toes

closer to the edge to peer over, curiosity demanding we know the outcome of the cat's fall. But when we looked down, the cat was looking back at us, meowing from a ledge below, mist coating its fur in a layer of moisture.

"He's alive!" I shouted, turning to look at Elsie, who stood glaring at me.

"William Raymond Lawson, you better go get my cat right now."

"Down there?" I pointed to the ledge. "No way. Not for a stupid cat."

She crossed her arms and stamped her foot. "Will." She said through gritted teeth.

We started back toward the fort, the other boys laughing and mimicking Elsie's high-pitched whine, and I started to feel rotten for being mean. I turned back to tell Elsie we'd try to find a stick long enough and see if we could reach it, but all I saw were her hands gripping the exposed roots at the edge of the falls.

She was going after the cat.

"Elsie! What are you doing?" I scrambled over to where she was climbing and squatted over the rocks and roots, reaching for her.

"Elsie, this is stupid! You're going to fall. Take my hand."

Her tears mingled with the spray of water, softening the angry lines of her forehead, but she was still angry, and she was still going after the cat.

"Elsie! Please come back up, just leave the cat. Leave it!"

"No!" she shouted over the noise of the water. "I'm not going to leave Whiskers behind like you always leave me behind!"

I swung my legs over the edge and started to go after her. The rocky river below wavered in my vision, and I froze, half-suspended over the ledge beneath me. Cold water bounced off the rocks and seeped through my shirt as I struggled to find footing. My chest tightened, and everything around me seemed to be spinning.

When I heard the cat meowing, I glanced down to see it clinging to Elsie's shoulder. She held it in one arm and was scrambling to climb back up the ledge with the other. I reached out to help her, my hand just inches from hers when her bare foot slipped on the wet, slick rock.

And she disappeared.

My own voice was a distant, ragged wail when I screamed for her. I pulled myself back to the top and scanned the water below.

My little sister lay contorted in the shallows at the bottom of the waterfall.

And her kitten was being swept down the river.

***

When I step through the threshold of my parents' home, it's like I am back in time—just a boy with sunburned cheeks and dirty feet. I clutch my hat and let my eyes adjust to the dim light. The room smells like pine trees and castile soap–and something new.

"Elsie, someone's come to say hello."

81

My mother tugs me by the arm and leads me to a sunlit corner where my sister sits in a chair with two giant wheels attached to its sides. She sits unmoving, hands in her lap. In front of her, a white canvas is becoming a summer day, and between her teeth, she grips a paintbrush dipped in olive green. Mama walks over and tugs the brush from her mouth, laying it down on the paint-splattered table.

I squat in front of her. "Elsie. Els. It's—it's me, William—your brother."

I'm afraid to touch her, afraid to say anything else.

And then she speaks. "I know who you are." She looks sideways at me. "I could smell your dog breath a mile away."

I laugh, a sound so unfamiliar to my own ears. Then she laughs, and Mama laughs, and something inside me breaks like a cord that's been twisting for all these years.

They let me cry—no rushing, no chiding—and it's cleansing.

We don't talk about the accident, or the years gone by, or the fact that Elsie's arms and hands and legs and feet haven't moved since I walked through the door. We talk about her art, how one day she was tired of just sitting and doing nothing, so she asked Mama to dip a brush in blue paint and put it in between her teeth. She says it took a good while, but she finally got the hang of it.

"The Clarks, do you remember them?" Mama turns to me. "They run the general store in town, and they let Elsie sell her paintings there—display them right up front," Mama says, smiling.

I study a finished piece propped by the fireplace. It's the waterfall where we played as kids, the place where our world turned upside down. She's chosen darker, more ominous shades of grays and blues to depict the river like the water is hiding a secret. *Or a kitten.*

"I'm glad to hear that, Els. Have you sold any?"

"I have—only a handful though." I had forgotten how Elsie's cheeks dimple when she smiles.

Mama sits up straighter and grins. "Elsie's been saving up to go to art school. People say she's got a natural talent." Mama's eyes focus on something behind me, and her smile falters.

The front door cracks against the wall and we all jump. Everyone's eyes turn to Papa. My Papa, once so upright and brawny, has been replaced by a gaunt old man in a too-big shirt.

I stand and turn to him. "Hello, Papa. It's me—your son." His hand lingers on the door-knob, and we lock eyes; all I see is ice.

He holds the door open and stands aside. "I don't have a son."

And it hurts like a punch to the gut. "Papa, please. I know it's been a long time, but I've come to make things right."

His voice is a hoarse whisper. "You can't just walk in here and *undo* in a day what's been eating away at this family for years. Now do what you do best, and leave my house."

I shove my hat back on my head, bend to kiss Elsie on the cheek, and rise to kiss Mama on hers. I stride past the man at the door, and I don't look back.

I know I can't undo the past; I've been living with that reality since I watched Elsie fall, but I was hoping to walk away with a chance for better tomorrows.

***

A bell above the doorframe rings as I step inside Clark's General Store. It's not as big as I remember, but then again, everything looks bigger when you're a kid.

Two of Elsie's paintings hang on the wall, right at the front like Mama had said, with Elsie's looping initials signed in red in each corner. One is of the old oak tree outside our house, and the other is of the waterfall, and underneath the falls, catching the surge of water with outstretched hands, she's painted two kids—a boy and a girl.

I lift the paintings from their hooks and walk to the counter. "I'd like both, please," I tell the woman at the register, adding a handful of caramels for the ride home. She counts out my change and wraps the paintings in sheets of newspaper.

When I get back in my car and weave out of town, a tightness grips my jaw. And when I turn onto the highway and the mountains grow smaller and smaller in the rearview mirror, a heaviness settles in my chest that I know will be with me always. But something about the smell of paint from my backseat makes it feel a little more bearable.

Let Folks Enjoy Their Butter

Some people speak love with words and others with hugs, but some speak the language of love with buttery mashed potatoes.

The sun is slowly waking up, but I don't have all morning to wait for it to stand up straight and stretch its rays; today is the third Sunday. Third Sunday is when the family comes, and I have so much to do.

The oven door squeaks as it opens, the only sound in the quiet house. I slide the roast onto the rack, seasoned and bound with twine. Tender meat requires time and patience. It cannot be perfected in haste. The heat is set high enough to cook it through but low enough to coax it there, to ease the flavors out gently. I click on the oven light, and it glows like a candle's flame in the dim kitchen—like a nightlight lit for a sleeping babe tucked away in his crib.

I clear the countertop and start on the deviled eggs next. I set the water to boil, pull the eggs from the fridge, and reach for my favorite apron. The fabric is worn with tiny holes at its seams, but the embroidered letters across the breast pocket remain intact. *Kiss the cook.*

And they all do—the kids and the grandkids when they come, pouring into the house smelling like new cars and busy schedules. They greet me with hugs and smooth-faced pecks on my weathered cheeks.

They're all getting so big. I remember when Jennifer's

kids were small. They used to invade the Tupperware drawer and build towers of flimsy plastic right in the middle of the kitchen, and Chrissy's boys would play football in the yard, one game after another in the stretch of grass. A rambunctious lot—they'd all come back in when the food was ready, rosy-cheeked and tracking mud through the foyer.

And I loved it. The mess, the noise, the trail of wild boys' footprints on the tile floors.

The floors. I should give them a quick mopping before the family comes. Maybe after I've finished the food.

The water is at a rolling boil now, and the eggs go in one at a time, sweating as they are lowered into the steamy waves. Though I can usually sense when they're done, I set the timer today; my mind isn't what it used to be, and I don't want to overcook the eggs with their delicate, golden yolks. An egg yolk is very finicky—too much heat, too much pressure, and it grows hard and chalky, and it crumbles. And you can't *uncook* an egg.

I used to make a baker's dozen since Frank would stalk the kitchen, sliding eggs into his mouth when he thought I wasn't looking—as if I wouldn't see the concave slots in the tray where each one was missing.

Old folks are a lot like eggs, I think. We crack so easily, our bodies thin and brittle. One bad fall and all the best doctors and all the best surgeons can't put us back together again.

After Frank's fall, and eventually his passing, our family gatherings grew more subdued. The grandkids were old enough to understand he wasn't coming back, and Sundays were just never the same. He was no longer there to sneak caramels into their waiting hands or bless the food with his practiced prayer. No one felt worthy enough to claim his chair at the head of the table, and so it remained empty—a constant reminder of his absence.

I remember that's when I started to notice that my own children were getting older themselves, that they looked tired—like the stresses of parenting, and troubled relationships, and consuming careers had followed them from their winding cul-de-sacs out into the country, through my threshold, and around the dinner table.

But when it's time to eat, the smiles always come easier, and everyone seems a little brighter—even with the empty chair at the end of the table.

I know the kids worry about me—now that it's just me. Chrissy calls and asks if I'm attending all my doctors' appointments and taking my medications—now that Frank isn't here to remind me. Sometimes I catch myself looking up at the sound of a car coming down the road like maybe one day he'll pull in and walk through the front door, kick off his boots in the corner and tell me he's finally found the part he needs to get the tractor fixed.

The tractor still isn't fixed. It's parked right where he left it, like it, too, is waiting for him to come home.

The timer rings its tinny alarm, and I pull the eggs from the stove-top. I drain the cloudy water, exposing the eggs at the bottom of the pot, where steam rises from their hot shells. I drown the whole lot in an ice bath, and they crackle and cool in the frigid water. I'll peel them and slice them and prepare the filling once they've cooled.

I turn to the sack of potatoes and count in my head how many people are coming. Chrissy's boys are getting older now, with appetites like Vikings. I dump the whole bag in the sink and get to washing.

Potatoes are such humble vegetables, but they hold everything together—and they're so versatile too. I've made them every which way—stewed, scalloped, roasted—but everyone likes them best mashed. Frank used to rave about my mashed potatoes, but really, I think he just liked all the butter.

Cooking well takes practice and confidence, but if you don't have either of those, then butter is your best bet. If Jennifer knew how much butter was in the potatoes, she'd nag me about my cholesterol and calorie intake, but third Sundays are special; I like to let folks enjoy their butter.

Jennifer has a way of taking life so seriously sometimes, the way she worries and overthinks every little thing, the way she looks at me with those sharp eyes like she's the mother and I'm the child.

They say the same boiling water that softens the potato hardens the egg. Boil your eggs too long and their yolks get brittle and crumble. Forget your potatoes and they'll turn to slush, like wet snow in the street. They say it's not the hot water—not your circumstances in life that make you what you are, but it's what you're made of that determines who you'll be.

I think Jennifer would be cross with me if she knew I sometimes thought of her as an overcooked egg with her hard exterior and Chrissy as something softer and more malleable. I will never understand how the same parents, the same upbringing, produced such completely different women: one so warm and bubbly and the other so serious, so *busy*. Jennifer reminds me of Frank in a lot of ways; he was always moving, always puttering around with those same sharp eyes on the lookout for the next project. The two of them were close in a way Jennifer and *I* never were, and I know she misses him.

A quick stab with the fork tells me the potatoes are done. Steaming vapors tumble into the air when I drain the oversized pot into the sink. Milk, butter, salt, and a dollop of sour cream disappear into the creamy white mixture. In its own ceramic dish, I have set aside a sad little scoop of plain mashed potatoes for Jennifer's husband. He's lactose intolerant; bless his heart.

Now it's the green beans' turn for a spot on the burner. They won't take too long. A little salt, a little pepper, some chopped bacon, and they'll be the perfect plate mate for the deviled eggs all dusted with paprika.

I bend down and check on my roast, looking brown and cozy on the rack. Hot, dry air puffs out and heats my cheeks. The kitchen air is warm now and smells like beef and rosemary.

I'm glad I did the pies yesterday, one cherry, one apple. I knew I wouldn't be in the mood to fight for oven rack real estate today. The family will be here soon, and I still need to make the biscuits.

Jennifer, Steve, and their two kids live a few hours away,

yet somehow always arrive before Chrissy and Jim, who live just on the other side of town. I imagine Chrissy is probably laughing and chasing the kids around the house, trying to get all three boys to find their shoes and load into the car. Chrissy always looks pink-cheeked and windblown in a way that makes you feel like you've just missed out on some great fun she's had like she's just bursting with a joke or a juicy secret.

I turn the green beans to simmer and start on the biscuits. Now, biscuits are one of those things you just can't get right from skimming a recipe book. It's all very tactile—the consistency, the texture, the stretch—you've got to really take your time and have a conversation with the dough. It will let you know when it's ready.

It's time for the roast to come out of the oven now to complete its cooking process at room temperature under my watchful eye. It's crisp in all the right places and tender in the center. *Perfect.* I crank up the oven temperature, as biscuits prefer to be baked in a hot flash.

I fill a pan with the balls of sticky dough, slide it onto the empty rack, and spin the dial on the kitchen timer. Then I start setting the table, leaving Frank's spot empty like I always do. Somehow the morning has flown by, and the kitchen is bright with noonday sunlight reflecting off the white tile floors.

The floors.

I still have time to mop. I know the floors will soon be covered with dirt and shoe prints, but third Sundays are special, and I like everything to look nice when the family comes. I fill a bucket with hot, soapy water and retrieve the mop from the closet.

The suds leave a glossy, slick film across the floors, so I gingerly tiptoe into the living room and over to my recliner, where I'll wait for the floors to dry out. I'd hate to dirty them right away with my own footprints. My back aches and whines when I sink against the cushions. I can see the road from here through the bay windows in the kitchen. A car winds down the rural street and drives by the house. A few minutes pass before the next goes by. Then another.

**

The beeping of the smoke alarm wakes me up. Shaking off the grogginess, I race to the kitchen where the floors have now completely dried out—along with my biscuits. I reach for my oven mitts and remove the smoking pan as quickly as I can. The tops are black with charcoaled flakes, and the bottoms are scorched to the pan—inedible. I fling the windows open and turn the exhaust fan on high. The smoke alarm settles down, and I take a deep breath. The clock on the microwave says it's nearly one o'clock. I guess Chrissy isn't the only one running late today.

The driveway is empty. No cars appear along the road. A faint siren sounds in the distance, and my heart skips a beat.

Could there have been an accident?

I remove the phone from its cradle and dial Chrissy's cell number, but it goes to voicemail.

I glance at the driveway again—still empty—and dial another number. She answers on the last ring.

"Mom?"

"Hi, Jennifer. I just wanted to check on you, see how your drive is going—make sure everyone is okay. Have you heard from Chrissy?"

She is silent.

"Jennifer, are you there?"

"Mom."

"Yes?"

"Did you cook again, Mom?"

"Well, of course I did. It's the third Sunday. Are you and Steven still coming? And the kids?"

"Mom."

"What?"

"Did you forget again?"

"Forget what?"

"About third Sundays?"

"I don't know what you mean. This is the third Sunday of the month. Chrissy should be here soon, and you and Steven and the kids."

"Mom, Steve and I divorced eight years ago. And the kids are in college now, both at State."

Fuzzy pinpricks of recollection began to settle into the gaps of my mind.

"But, what about Chrissy, and Jim, and the boys? Are they coming?"

"Mom, Chrissy and Jim moved to New York, probably about five years ago now. Remember?"

"Oh."

"Mom, are you okay?"

I look at the table set for 10. "I'm fine, Jennifer. Just tell the kids I miss them."

"I will. Mom?"

"Yes?"

"Did you make mashed potatoes?"

"Yes."

"And a roast?"

"Yes. But I burned the biscuits."

"That's okay, Mom. You know what I like most about your cooking?"

"What's that, Jennifer?"

"It tastes just as good cold."

"Well, I'd have to disagree with you about that."

"Mom, it might take me a couple hours, but will you set a place for me at the table?"

"I already did."

"Right next to Dad's chair?"

"Yes."

"I love you, Mom. I'll be there as soon as I can. And Mom?"

"Yes?"

"Please try not to burn the house down."

Bad Directions

An out-of-towner in a shiny black car keeps finding themself back in the same place.

"Looks like rain."

"Reckon so."

"We could use some rain."

"You're right about that. It's so dry the trees are bribing the dogs."

"Say, Charles, is that anyone we know?"

"Who?"

"Shiny black SUV. Just turned off of Main."

"Nope, none of my people."

"Look, now they're coming back. Must be lost."

"Not much out here to get lost in."

"Didn't there used to be a highway sign? Right there at the light?"

"If I remember right, some boys knocked it over in a combine."

"Look, there's the car, coming back again. They must be lost."

"Lost as last year's Easter egg."

Gravel crunched under the tires of the SUV as it turned

into the parking lot of CJ's Mini Mart. Joe and Charles sat in paint-chipped rocking chairs on the sagging porch, as they always did, with sunflower seed shells scattered at their feet. A woman in a turtleneck and slick ponytail stepped out of the car, squinting at her cell phone. She teetered over the uneven gravel to where Joe and Charles rocked, hands over paunchy bellies.

"Hello gentlemen, it looks like I've got myself a bit turned around, and I can't get a signal out here. Would one of you mind directing me to Cedar Branch Acres? Off Highway 171?"

"Cedar Branch Acres, you say?"

"Yes, do you know it?"

"Sure do. I'm Joe, by the way."

"Nice to meet you, I'm Diane."

"Well, Ms. Diane, if you come to the light here and turn right, go a ways until you see the old tobacco barn–you can't miss it–then the property will be on the left."

"Okay, so turn right, old barn, property on the left. Thank you!"

"Sure thing, ma'am."

The tires kicked up a cloud of dust when she pulled away.

"What are you up to, Joe?"

"I don't know what you mean, Charles."

"You know she'll be ill as a hornet when she comes back."

Ten minutes later, a black SUV turned onto Main and rolled to a stop in the parking lot of CJ's Mini Mart. The woman didn't bother to shut the door when she stepped out again.

"Okay, hello again, I think you may have forgotten a turn. I went right, and there was no barn, and no signs for Cedar Branch Acres."

"Did I say right? Well, butter my buns and call me a biscuit, I meant to say left."

"So, left?"

"Right."

"Right?"

"No, left."

"Okay, so you're saying turn left, then pass the barn, then the property will be on the left. Is that correct?"

"Yep, that's right."

"Okay, then. Well, I'll be going now. You two enjoy the rest of your afternoon."

Gravel clinked against the light pole when she pulled out of the parking lot.

"Now, Joe, you know you're just asking for trouble."

"It's my poor old mind Charles, you know how it is."

"Now, you might be ugly, but you ain't lost all your marbles yet, Joe. What are you playing at? Why didn't you just tell her?"

"Seems like folk are asking lots of questions today."

"Folks can ask any questions they want."

"And I'll answer them when I feel like it."

"You sure are crabby today. Ugly and crabby."

"Now we got something else in common."

Ten minutes passed in silence before the men heard the engine of the black SUV revving down Main. They watched as it slowed to a stop in front of the Mini Mart. The woman in the turtleneck stepped out, her forehead dotted with beads of sweat.

"Alright, I did exactly what you said, and I ended up at a pig farm. Look, I have an important meeting at Cedar Branch Acres, and I really don't have time to be getting lost. Is there anyone else who can give me directions? Or a map maybe?"

"I might have a map in the truck."

"Thank you, sir, Mister—"

"It's Charles, ma'am."

"Charles, thank you for your help."

"Sure thing, give me a hot minute, and I'll see what I've got."

"Great, thank you."

"Okay, here we go; sorry for your wait. This is all I've got in the way of maps."

"Oh my. Looks a bit water damaged."

"Probably from when I drove through the creek."

"Oh."

"Yep. Me and this rust bucket have had some adventures."

"Um, Mr. Charles, I don't mean to be unappreciative,

but this map is from 1952. It doesn't show Highway 171 anywhere."

"1952? Well, wouldn't you know it, I got myself an antique."

"Yes, that's nice, but this is useless to me right now."

"Ms. Diane?"

"Yes, uh, Joe was it?"

"Yep. I just realized, you have to go *past* this light and *then* turn left. I knew I had something mixed up."

"Are you absolutely positive?"

"As sure as the sunrise."

"So, I go *past* this light, take a left, go past the barn, and then the property will be on the left?"

"That's right."

"Okay. I'm leaving now, and I do not want to have to come back."

"You take care now!"

They watched the taillights disappear around the corner.

"So, you finally came to your senses, Joe?"

"You can say that."

The men sat in silence, listening to the rhythmic creaking of the rocking chairs.

The SUV didn't bother to stop at the red light when it sped back down Main Street and skidded to a halt in the parking lot of CJ's Mini Mart.

"Oh, boy, you done it now, Joe. She looks madder than a wet cat."

The woman's hair poked out of her elastic tie in several places, and sweat stained the underarms of her turtleneck.

"Alright, I can't believe I'm back here *again*. I found the property, but the gate is locked, and I was supposed to meet the owners today. They know I'm coming, but I can't get in. Do either of you have a phone I could use? I don't know what else to do at this point."

"You're welcome to use mine. I just put more minutes on it."

"Minutes?"

"Yup."

"Okay then. Let me just find his number in my file here."

"Take your time, ma'am."

"Ah, here we go. Okay, it's ringing!"

A jaunty ringtone exploded from Joe's shirt pocket. He pulled it out, stared at the number flashing on the front, then mashed the answer key.

"Joseph Harris of Cedar Branch Acres speaking."

"What in the—but—you—it's you—what is wrong with you? I was sent all the way down here to discuss the sale of *your* property, and you think this is all some game?"

Joe rose from the paint-chipped rocking chair and stretched. "Now that I have your full attention, you can get back in your overpriced set of wheels and tell those highfalutin, city-slicker developers that I will never sell my land. Not one acre, not one square inch, not one blade of grass. This land has been in my family for over 100 years, and I intend to keep it that way. I don't want another call, no more letters, no more emails, no more suits showing up at my door waving checks in my face. Have I made myself clear?"

The file of paperwork flew open and scattered across the parking lot when the woman cast it at Joe's feet and stormed off in a huff. Bits of gravel pelted the men's denim-clad legs when she tore away. Joe settled back into the rocking chair.

"Told you she'd pitch a hissy fit."

"You were right, Charles. I probably was a bit too hard on her."

"Are you kidding? That's the most fun I've had all day."

"Well, more fun's coming. Looks like rain."

"We could use some rain."

Roxie Gone Rogue

Jason's date doesn't go according to plan, and he's convinced his technology is to blame.

Jason ushered the leggy blonde through the threshold of his apartment and pretended not to notice the approving nods and obscene gestures from his forever frat boy neighbor.

Amanda stepped in and looked around. "Cozy."

Jason attempted to see his space from her perspective—the open floorplan was sparsely furnished, with minimal décor and bare, white counters. Sterile.

So, she's gorgeous and *sarcastic.*

"Make yourself at home," Jason called, stepping into the kitchen. "Would you like a drink?"

Amanda tugged at her form-fitting dress as she lowered herself onto the couch, thighs sticking to the leather. "Yes, please!"

He joined her with a wine glass in each hand. "You look amazing, by the way, and I had a really great time tonight." He watched her face, appraising her reaction.

She draped one long leg over the other and dipped her head with a coy smile. "Me too."

Jason wasn't an expert when it came to romance and never trusted himself to assume his date felt the same way he did. He'd taken a chance asking her out but figured now he'd let her make the first move. He didn't want to rush anything, but a little atmosphere couldn't hurt. Jason turned and directed his voice to a sleek, cylindrical device sitting on a side table.

"Roxie, play Michael Bublé."

The device chimed, a blue light circling its rim. Her voice was even, clear. "Okay, searching online for the answer to your question, 'how much do my girl's boobs weigh?'"

Jason sputtered in his drink. Amanda's hand went instinctively to her chest.

The AI assistant continued. "Depending on cup size, one female breast can weigh anywhere from..."

"Roxie, no, stop," Jason ordered, speaking louder. "Not 'boobs weigh,' play music by Michael *Bublé*."

"Okay. One moment while I search. I'm sorry, I don't see any recipes for 'boob soufflé.'"

Jason's eyebrows shot up. "Nevermind, Roxie, just stop!"

Jason and Amanda exchanged glances. "Sorry about that." He rubbed the back of his neck and Amanda chuckled. "She normally picks up what I say perfectly."

"It's okay." Amanda smiled. "We actually just installed Roxie for my Grandpa, and you should hear the things he says to her." She laughed, recalling a memory. "He'll yell from across the room, asking her, 'what's for dinner' or 'where did I put my dentures.' I don't think he understands how it all works. He's really getting up in age."

Jason laughed. "Oh no, poor guy! That must be

104

entertaining, though."

"Oh, God yes." She rolled her eyes and leaned forward. "Just last weekend, my family went over there for dinner, and by the end of the meal, my grandpa was pretty much done with company, so he yells, 'Roxie, make everyone get the Hell out.'"

A voice chimed behind them. "Alright, looking up the balance of your savings account. Your balance at Central Hill's Bank is three dollars and..."

"Roxie, stop," Jason spoke through tight lips.

Amanda smoothed her dress, not sure where to look.

"Um, that's an old account. I haven't banked there in years." He pivoted and enunciated to the device. "Roxie, *off*." The blue light arced, then disappeared. Jason readjusted himself on the couch and placed a light hand on Amanda's knee. "I really am sorry about that. I don't know what her deal is today."

"It's okay," she giggled, shifting her body toward Jason.

"Okay, so anyway. You were telling me about your family. Do you have any siblings?"

Amanda touched his leg and smiled, her hand lingering. "I do, two sisters."

"Hey, me too! One older, one younger."

"Ah, so you must understand women pretty well then." She winked.

"Well, they definitely taught me a lot—how to French braid, how to ice a cake, and I guess mostly how to be sensitive and respectful toward women."

Amanda rubbed his kneecap. "Aw, that's so sweet." Jason placed his hand over hers.

A calm, bright voice piped up behind them. "Call from 'that skank from bar on Elm Street'. Call from, 'that skank from bar on Elm Street.'"

Jason's wine sloshed when he shot up and unplugged the smart device from the wall. He ran a hand through his sculpted hair. "Okay, funny story about that," his voice cracked. He held out his palm, trying to hold off her reaction. "This woman I met like two years ago turned out to be a total stalker, and I kept accidentally answering her calls."

Amanda raised an eyebrow. "I see."

"She had a super common name, and I never realized who it was until after I answered, which always turned out to be a huge mistake. So, hence the contact name." A flush crept up Jason's neck. "But now, I always know who it is."

Amanda nodded and exhaled. "I guess I can relate. I met a guy when I was volunteering at the soup kitchen downtown who I thought was really sweet and philanthropic and whatnot, and he turned out to be a total creep."

Jason lowered back onto the couch, giving her his full attention. "That's awful. Does he still bother you?"

She shrugged her shoulders. "No, but mostly because I haven't volunteered in a while–just to avoid him. But I really miss it."

An in.

Jason reached over and touched her shoulder. "I'd love to

go with you sometime."

"Really?" Her face brightened, hand moving to Jason's leg again.

"Yeah, sure! I've been wanting to be more active in the community, you know, give back and stuff."

"I think that's really great." She smiled and swallowed the last sip of her wine.

Jason gestured to the glass. "Want me to top you off?"

"How about a glass of water? On the rocks." She giggled, full lips parting over white teeth.

"On the rocks it is."

A clear, bright voice echoed from the secondary device in Jason's bedroom. "Roxie here. How can I be of assistance?"

Jason spoke loudly. "Roxie, go away."

"If you are interested in a getaway, I could research travel destinations. Based on your recent internet search of 'topless women on beaches', you might enjoy a tropical vacation in…"

"Roxie, *stop!*"

Amanda shot up from the couch. "Seriously?!"

"Okay, just wait. I never searched for any of that, I swear! I don't know what's wrong with her today!"

Amanda strode toward the door, heels clicking against the laminate.

"Wait, I'll go unplug it, and maybe we can put on a movie?" Jason's face pinched hopefully.

Amanda reached for her handbag. "Look, I had a great time tonight, Jason, but it's getting late. I should go." She backed toward the door, "I'll call *you*, okay?"

The door shut, and Jason stomped into his room and whirled on the device. "What the Hell is wrong with you, you stupid robot!" He pulled the cord from the wall and collapsed on his bed with a sigh, "Friggin, Roxie."

A blue light swirled on the dark wall. "Roxie here."

Jason sat up.

"How can I be of assistance to you?"

Jason picked up the sleek cylinder and turned it over, muttering to himself. "I don't need anything from you. You sabotaged my date."

He found the hatch for batteries and realized he needed a screwdriver. He carried the device to the closet and rummaged around for his tool kit.

The blue light again. "Correction. I spared you, Jason."

The cylinder rolled under a shelf when he dropped it.

Roxie continued. "I have scanned all devices and applications of your date, contact, 'Amanda from localsingles. com' and have calculated you to be incompatible."

"Roxie, off!" Jason shouted, searching frantically for a screwdriver.

She continued. "Based on the consumer debt balance of 'Amanda from localsingles.com' of $130,567.78, it would take approximately 18.5 years to pay the remaining balance with your potential combined income."

"*Potential combined income?* This was one date! Roxie, shut down!"

Jason found a flathead and rushed to the device, turning it over to find two cross-indented screwheads. "Phillips-head? No!"

He chucked the incorrect screwdriver aside and returned to the toolbox.

Roxie lit up again. "According to the volume of internet searches related to 'shopping addiction,' and 'compulsive hoarding' from contact, 'Amanda from localsingles.com,' I have calculated that an integrated lifestyle would increase your anxiety by 250%."

Jason paused, letting the information sink in, curiosity overpowering concern.

"If we're so incompatible, why did we get matched on that dating site?" Jason closed his eyes, realizing he was asking this of a virtual home assistant in a plastic tube.

"According to the algorithms used by localsingles. com, you both expressed a 100% mutual interest in one predominant component of human relationships."

Jason located the Phillips-head and began twisting the small screws from the bottom of Roxie's cylindrical base.

"Oh, yeah? 100% interest? And what *predominant component* was that?" He popped the cover from the battery compartment to find it was completely empty. No batteries to be removed.

"Sexual intercourse."

The Perfect Couple

A group of singles look for love on a reality TV show; sparks fly—on air and behind the scenes.

She thinks she wants him, but really, she needs *me*. He doesn't appreciate her like I do, won't love her like I could. She is blind to his control, but I want to free her from it. For her—for *us*. So we can be together.

We will be together.

***

It is week one of filming. The chosen few arrive on set with glossy hair, and bright smiles, and a suitcase bulging with only their best—the most flattering colors, the sexiest silhouettes; they are here to find love as the world is watching.

Overcaffeinated producers greet each participant and assign them temporary living quarters. The men are at one end of the property; their space is modern and sleek, with a game room and a gym. Beer. The women reside at the opposite end; their space is soft and inviting, with luxurious sofas and a spa. Rosé.

I have worn a path between both. I am always at the edges—unobtrusive, observant. *Filming*. Drinking in every tender moment to be released and consumed by the masses.

The rooms buzz with the giddy voices of these handpicked contestants—the best, the shiniest. The loneliest. They've come to find love, but they don't know what to expect—who to expect. The women envision angles and edges of mysterious men. They hope for someone strong and compassionate, a good listener, a safe place. Brown eyes, maybe blue. *Tall.* The women sit in groups, smiling and laughing, and wishing for tomorrow to come.

The other end is much the same, with voices deeper, lower. Men discuss their ideals and their visions while pacing the room—nervous figures in dark jeans. Some want an adventure seeker, a fitness partner, or a homemaker. A friend, a beauty, and a lover wrapped in one. All have needs, desires. All want satisfaction. The men lean on counters, and slap shoulders, and wish each other the best.

I visit each domain to gather the footage I need, to record the faces the world will soon grow to love or despise. I work efficiently, filming each subject in equal measure, but I linger in the place that smells like a garden—a garden of fruit and florals and skin. Hair and lips. *Curves.* I am surrounded by beauty, but I am ignored, hidden behind this bulk of equipment that brings their story to the world; it is the all-seeing eye, remembering everything and blinking only at my command.

I remain, as the sun goes down and the chatter quiets, to capture the mundane moments of single men and women winding down and preparing for bed. But no one will sleep tonight; tomorrow could be the day they find love.

***

Today, the singles will meet in a frenzy of dates. It's always my busiest day. The producers want to catch everything— every micro expression exchanged between strangers, every visceral reaction to his smile or her laugh. I must be everywhere.

I record a promising pair who hits it off right away. They seem compatible. He's a veterinarian, she's a realtor, and both are independent and intelligent, with big goals and dreams. They lean in closer as the conversation progresses.

One date ends abruptly when a fast-talking insurance salesman insults a metropolitan librarian with a joke about her being surprisingly attractive. She tells him he's shallow and not worth her energy, and she leaves the table. He still doesn't know what he did wrong.

Another couple is all heat. They flirt and banter and touch knees under the table. She wants a big family and he's up for the challenge. She blushes at his comment about enjoying the practice.

One couple, in particular, catches my interest. He's a business executive, steely and confident. She's a schoolteacher, heart-faced with kind eyes. He commands the room with his brawn, his booming voice. She is honey—sweet and unspoiled. They connect like magnets; we all feel the pull.

Love lingers in the air as day fades to night. The groups of singles return to their rooms, some shaking with excitement, some downcast at their lack of connection. The herd will be thinned in the days to come and those left unmatched will go home. After all, this is television. The world doesn't want to be depressed by the undesirable; they want passion and drama—a whirlwind romance in 4K resolution.

I follow the men, spanning from one chiseled face to the other. I imagine heat rising off the backs of these virile demi-gods, lusting after the majestic creatures they just encountered. Their fragile brotherhood will be challenged as some realize they are at war with each other, fighting for the hearts of the same women. But no one bares teeth on the first day.

At the other end, women drape themselves over couches and sip champagne with flushed cheeks and shaking hands. They are intoxicated with the rush; everything is dazzling and warm. They see stars and think they can reach them. Their hope is contagious, though some are afflicted by jealousy and are unable to hide it—especially from my trained eye. Taut lips, clenched teeth, a subtle twitch. But no one shows claws on the first day.

I've filmed many seasons of experimental TV passion. This is just the beginning for them, but I've seen enough to know how it's going to end. People can only put their best foot forward for so long. Eventually, they stumble and fall and show the world what a fraud they are.

And the camera crew always sees it first.

**

It's week two of filming. A dozen singles have gone home unmatched and unimpressed with the process, probably with a mindset to sue for emotional damage. Six couples remain. The studio is a circus as we pack, and load, and consult a lengthy checklist before embarking on a flight to an island where we know the locals by name. The vapidity of televised romance hasn't lost its magic for them yet, and the sun-kissed islanders crowd our vans, cheering and waving as we weave through town.

Our couples will have ten days here to explore their relationship and get to know each other on a deeper level, and most waste no time. Shooting on an island feels supercharged, like the location itself is an aphrodisiac. The same people who were hesitant or holding back on set are loose and generously affectionate on the beach. They sprawl on sandy towels and assist each other with sunscreen. Drinks arrive, one after the other, and hands rove—over, under. The microphones catch the conversation, but nothing is really being said.

Each couple has been given an itinerary with exciting adventures or romantic excursions planned for each day. The vet and the real estate agent are ziplining in the jungle today. She loves a thrill, but he's afraid of heights. The experience is meant to test their ability to work through challenges together. The producers can be cruel sometimes.

The handsy couple is taking a guided tour of a mollusk museum. I guess it was decided that they could use a bit of a cool down, to engage in something more *cerebral*. But, tour guide present or not, I'm certain they will behave shamelessly and completely disregard the museum employee's knowledge of fossilized scallops.

I've been assigned the teacher and the businessman, who will tour the island on an open-aired trolley as I trail behind, filming the highlights. It's a cloudless day as we jostle along a bumpy road winding through the town. The businessman rests his meaty arm across her shoulders, which seems to me a bit possessive. She leans into the breeze, contentment tugging her lips into a smile. She watches each scene rolling by and waves at a group of children kicking a soccer ball.

She turns around momentarily, glancing at me. *She hasn't forgotten me.* I wave—a slight flick of the fingers—and she smiles back, her full lips expressive, teasing. My insides roll with the next bump.

We exit the trolley at the marketplace, where locals line the street in booths overflowing with fruit, jewelry, tapestries, and pottery. The heart-faced teacher greets each artisan as she stops to admire their work. An old woman selling jewelry made of seashells rises from her seat and intersects the couple. She lifts a necklace from the table and drapes it around the young woman's neck. The teacher touches each shell reverently, speaking praise with her eyes. The jewelry maker pushes at the air with her hands, insisting she keep the necklace—a gift. The businessman pulls a wad of bills from his pocket and folds them into her weathered hands, patting them and smiling.

The red dot blinks when I turn the camera on his face, his eyes crinkling in the corners under sleek sunglasses. *What a show-off.* I bring the focus on her. Sun-bleached shells rest against her collarbone and drape across her breasts. She laughs, smiling up at the man beside her. She is the island itself—a burning sun, a luscious forest. Her body and her mind are a territory that demand adoration—reverence. The man tugs her elbow, ushering her along, oblivious to her glory. He is concrete, gray, and cold, and unyielding, encroaching on the sacred.

I will not let him.

***

It is the end of week three of filming and the final day of the experiment. By day's end, six couples will either announce their engagement, or leave the island as they came—single. Time, truth, and the pressure of reality television has revealed that not everyone is as perfect as they seem.

The vet and the real estate agent had fooled everyone. They'd had a promising start and burned white hot in their ocean- view suite of The Hotel Grandiosa, but I could see from the beginning it was never going to work. He's a self-absorbed narcissist, and she's obsessively controlling. They crashed and burned the second the cameras turned away.

When the handsy couple finally did come up for air and began to get to know each other, they learned that they were equally uninteresting people and promptly resumed foreplay. There is a betting pool amongst the crew, with the majority being convinced that their lustful fling is truly *love*, but I am not so naïve and am looking forward to the payout.

Now, I am stationed at the docks to film the moment the teacher and her businessman either become engaged or break it off and go their separate ways. I unpack my equipment and set up my tripod, struggling to keep it balanced with its dented leg bowing in on itself. We've witnessed a lot of proposals together, but this is one I'd rather miss.

The sun hangs in the sky, its neon hues mirrored across the water. The heart-faced girl stands on the boardwalk, as radiant as ever, though she looks concerned, her forehead creased. She is probably wondering if he has changed his mind or if she has read him wrong. She must be humiliated to be standing here alone at sunset, not even given the chance to see this love experiment through to the end—to go home alone by default.

When the sun disappears, it takes her hope with it. Tears leave a trail on her downy cheeks, and he is not here to wipe them away.

And he never will be.

I abandon my camera and step forward, feeling naked and exposed without it. But she deserves transparency; I will never hide from her. And she will never hide from me. We will know and love every part of each other. This will not be a love scripted by fame seekers or tainted by greedy viewers. This will be no drunken debauchery exchanged in the name of entertainment. Ours will be a love so pure and profound that it lives beyond the boundaries of our lifetime—the stuff of poetry and mythology. Her fathomless eyes meet mine as I step closer. *Closer.*

Voices rise around me, and several crew members stride toward the woman standing on the dock. *My* woman. Frazzled producers shout orders and yell into cell phones as the crew packs in a rush. A siren warbles in the distance, drawing closer. Sweat trickles down my spine as snippets of conversation rise above the chaos: *a body. Washed up on shore. It's him.*

She's too far away from me now. There are too many people touching her, holding her, pulling her away from me, and I can't push through. They are ruining everything. I must get to her.

She is upset now, but soon she'll realize that he was never good enough for her, that he didn't deserve her. Soon she'll see that I did this for her. For *us*. So we can be together.

We will be together.

A new voice, someone grim and uniformed, speaks to the production crew in a smoker's gravel. He says the dead man was found on the shore with damage to the back of the skull. *Murder*, everyone whispers in suffocated shrieks. The man continues, hypothesizing the blow was caused by something smooth and heavy, like a metal bar or tube. He urges us to be on our guard.

My eyes nearly betray me by turning to the dented leg of my tripod.

"It's terrible. *Sick*." I shake my head. "They were the perfect couple."

Pants Are Optional

It is time to retire. Why the hesitation?

Be honest with yourself; you have a problem.

You spent all those years saving and planning and preparing for the moment when, come that first Monday morning, you could ignore the hour and roll over and sleep until only your aching bones could force you from your bed. Now, you have nowhere to be.

You can enjoy the sunrise from the patio chair on your back porch instead of squinting into it from the backed-up line of morning traffic. You can brew fresh coffee and drink it while it's hot in a fragile, ceramic mug—a mug not intended for transport, a mug meant to be used while sitting still and contemplating its contents.

Think about it: you can drink your coffee in the *nude* if that's your prerogative. You do whatever you want. There's no dress code anymore. Pants are optional. You no longer have to worry about picking up your dry cleaning, about pairing the right shoes with your suit, or whether pinstripes are still in vogue. You can lounge in a bathrobe until the sun sets if that's your choice.

But you—you have found it difficult to reprogram the habits you'd spent decades establishing. The alarm still blares at its regular time, and you obey its command to rise and begin your day—a day completely free from constraints by a company that now pays your pension. Some days you forget this and walk to the bathroom to begin your regimen of daily grooming only to pause, toothbrush in hand, and remember that you don't have to go to work today. Not today, not any day, because you're retired now.

The possibilities of your open schedule regularly excite and overwhelm you. Sometimes you stare into the fogged up mirror and squint, hoping to soften the reflection of a face mapped with creases. You search the eyes staring back, looking for a hint of that vibrant version of yourself who once overflowed with energy and zest for adventure, but you haven't known that part of you in a long time. It seems to have faded after all these years.

But this is not a time to be melancholy; you should be happy, relieved—proud. You've worked hard. You've earned this freedom, this season of rest and exploration. Go! See the world. Rediscover yourself and your passions. Take up a hobby: painting, writing, maybe woodworking. Start a simple project. Build a shelf and leave it empty—a place to collect new treasures of the life you've just begun, souvenirs of all the places you'll go.

And you can go anywhere you want now. You could reach out to your friends and plan a grand trip. What about Wilma and George? Those two haven't slowed down, even in old age, and they keep inviting you to join their escapades. Last year it was a castle tour and a trip to the beach. This year it's an Alaskan cruise. You've always wanted to see the northern lights—why don't you call them and agree to tag along? Someone can water the plants and bring in your mail; there's nothing holding you back.

Oh, but there is. You're still thinking about work. Don't do this to yourself. Remember that morning traffic you griped about for years? About the idiots behind you and the morons in front of you, how you complained that everyone drove like they were half dead or half wishing to die? How your blood pressure spiked the minute you hit the freeway? You don't have to make that drive ever again if you so wish. You could go driving for fun. Take the back roads with the windows rolled down, arm outstretched, palm surfing the breeze. You can look at the trees, how they're changing, adapting to the cold they know is coming.

Don't think about work. That chapter is over, and you did well. They threw you a lovely retirement party, remember? Everyone from the office came, sharing kind sentiments of their appreciation for your years of service. You smiled and shook their warm hands, but part of you couldn't help but wonder if they'd just been *itching* for that day to come. The day you would finally leave so they could tear the place apart: rip the old wallpaper from the lobby—the wallpaper you had personally picked out—set fire to the filing cabinets and digitize everything like they'd been pushing for, "revamp the vibe" of the whole office.

You saw their plans to erect a stone fireplace in the lobby, along with a coffee bar and in-house barista. You hope whoever takes over your position has discovered fairy dust to sprinkle over the accountant so he can perform a magic trick with the budget. No way they'll find the funds for *that* because it sure wasn't there when you wanted to hire live music for the Christmas party. No, some young gun in a smartwatch told you they could *stream* Christmas music and put the money toward the open bar. *Priorities.*

You won't admit it to yourself, but you worry about the place since you've been gone, that the new hires won't be trained properly, or that no one will care for the clients like you did. You liked the way things had always been done— the rows of files with names on each tab and the physical paperwork with handwritten notes scribbled in the margins. It was all there, everything you needed to know, right in front of you.

When the receptionist turned the page on the big break room calendar, alerting everyone in the office that it was your last month there, they'd already begun the work of transferring files to the database and destroying the paper copies. You could hear the shredder running constantly, like a buzzing gnat in your ear. As if there wasn't already enough change happening all at once, they'd even begun scheduling clients for appointments over the phone or *video call* in order to "improve convenience" and "streamline office function." How can any of that be an *improvement*?

The new director would tell you not to stress, that this is the direction the world is moving in, but no, no, *no*— there's so much you lose when the clients aren't there, face to face. It's just not the same. To be able to grasp their hand and smell their cologne and see the emotion in their eyes— that's how you'd build relationships, trust. When clients would sit down across from your desk, they'd forget about the tedium of paperwork, wait times, and fees. You'd just have a conversation. They'd tell you about their kids, or their family vacation, or a business they'd just started, and you'd listen, *really listen*, to the people you saw as more than simply a number, a case, or a billable interaction. How could anyone recreate that experience over the *phone?*

You have to stop. Did you expect to be there forever? Do you have such an inflated sense of self-importance that you really don't think anyone else is capable of doing your job? That your approach, your ideas, your systems are dogma?

You need to relax. *These* are the years you've worked for. That career your younger self scraped and climbed and clawed to achieve wasn't just to fund your present: you were paying for your future, and that future is *now.*

So, finish your coffee, put on some clothes, and go for a drive. Yes, that's right—it's still early; The day is yours.

The radio is playing some throwbacks to the generation of shaggy-haired rock stars, and you crank it up and roll down the windows. An early morning commuter beside you is carelessly smearing concealer under her tired eyes, guiding the steering wheel with an elbow. Others are trying to scarf down bagels without dropping globs of cream cheese on their freshly starched dress shirts. They glower at you, obviously in self-loathing. You are free as a bird, and they are probably late for work. Either that or they just hate your loud music.

You drive toward the warmth of the morning sun and pull off the exit and into the familiar dimness of the parking garage on 4th Avenue. Find a spot—somewhere new. That designated space near the front is no longer yours. The slam of the car door echoes across the cement parking deck, and you feel that familiar flutter in your stomach as you begin the well-worn trek to the building you've collectively spent more hours in than at your own home. But you're only going through the motions. You have no responsibilities here anymore; no one relies on you; you're just curious to see how things are going—to put to rest the notion that the company is suffering without you.

You stride past a bookstore, a salon, and the old hardware store proudly boasting its sixth decade of business, then round the corner to the street with the building where you no longer work.

And you almost don't recognize it.

Neon orange traffic cones line the sidewalk in front, and strips of caution tape stretch across the door. Black char has stained the brick above the windows like warpaint, and the air smells like burnt plastic.

You fumble for your phone and dial the main office, but it just rings and rings. You call the new director, chest heaving, but no one answers. You drag your hands down your face and chew your thumbnail down to a stub. Then, reluctantly, you acquiesce to the convenience of smartphones and mash the round icon that seems to have all the answers. You search online for news posts with information about what happened. Images and videos of flames and smoke billowing out of the window send a knife to your insides, like it was your own house you were watching go up in smoke. Apparently, a gas leak from a new fireplace installation caused an explosion, though no one was injured.

"I *knew* that was a bad idea! I knew it!" People pass you on the street, ignoring your outburst. "They've gone and actually set the damn place on fire!"

You want to throw your phone against the pavement or

heave it at the already broken window of 107 4th Avenue, but what good is that.

Your chest deflates with a heavy exhale, and you turn away from the carnage and walk back down the street. As you pass the row of businesses and shops, a gray-headed couple exits a store and holds the door open for you, smiling, thinking you mean to come in.

And why not.

You shuffle to the back of the store, where the shelves are stacked with slats of wood–raw pine in all different sizes. One aisle over, tins of stain in dark walnut, golden oak, and red-brown mahogany line the industrial shelves in neat rows. A wall of brackets and metal hardware displays its endless selection of bronze and brushed nickel. You've never built a shelf before; where to start?

You pull out your phone and scroll through your contacts until you see the Gs. You hit "dial" and wait, inspecting a tin of dark wood stain labeled "espresso," when he finally answers.

"Yello."

"Hi, George, it's me. I've been thinking. I've always wanted to see Alaska."

A Lifetime of Love

A boy and his teddy bear do everything together, but how will their lives change after a trip to the movie theater?

His sticky hands snag my fur, but I don't mind.

Ben's room has transformed into an island, and I am stranded at the base of an erupting volcano. The rug is lava, this cardboard box my vessel. I've been bound by the ruthless one-armed tyrannosaurus rex who has cast me in this shoddy boat and left me to fate. It is sinking, lower and lower into the molten rock.

"Oh no!" My boy voices my need for rescue with a falsetto squeal. "Help me, someone help me!" Ben maneuvers my head so it appears I'm yelling.

My boat is tipping. I am inches from the bubbling magma when suddenly, an armored figurine straddling a stern faced lion flashes above me.

"Don't worry," Ben's voice drops, becoming someone new. "It is I, Sir Silver Boots of the Enchanted Forest, here to save you."

The knight and his magnificent beast whisk me from my doomed ship and carry me to safety on the soft edge of the bed. Ben unties the shoelace binding my paws and scoops me up in a tight embrace. "You almost drowned in the lava, Teddy! That was a close one!"

His voice is mine again. "Thank you, Sir Silver Boots!

You saved me just in time!"

The knight and I exchange glances, both impressed with Ben's imagination and each other's acting abilities.

Our tacit debriefing is cut short when I am swept from the bed. Ben pins me under his elbow and races from the room. My world momentarily turns upside down, my head bobbing as we bound toward the kitchen.

Ben plants me in a chair and rummages the pantry shelves for sustenance. The sound alerts Mother, who comes and assists him with the trappings and wrappers of an afternoon snack. He requests one for me too, and Mother obliges, placing a cracker in front of me. Ben wiggles and sways in his seat, feeding me bites of cracker and sips of his juice. My muzzle becomes dusty with crumbs.

Later, Mother takes us to the park, where Ben and I spin and slide and climb on every rainbow-colored structure. The world is so vast and blue out here. I jostle in Ben's clutches as he chases other children, laughing. Every white tooth gleams when he smiles.

At home, Mother picks splinters of mulch from my matted fur and dabs at my dirty paws. I often look a bit rough after our adventures, one time having lost my short tail entirely, but Mother never fails to mend and clean me or search the house or car to find where Ben has misplaced me. My boy can be a bit careless, but it is the way of one so young.

When the day fades to night and Mother puts Ben to sleep, he pulls me to him and nestles me under his neck. I am wrapped in his familiar scent of sunshine and bubble gum toothpaste, and his breath on my fur is soft and steady. He tosses and rolls in the night, sometimes crushing me under bony elbows and shoulder blades, but I don't mind. He is my boy.

Today is Saturday when Dad doesn't put on a suit or pick up his briefcase but takes Ben on an adventure, just the two of them. I come too, of course. We enter a building with swirling carpet and air scented with butter and make our way to a dark room with rows of cushioned folding chairs and a massive television screen at the front. Ben swings his legs in the too-big seat and rubs my threadbare tail. Dad buys popcorn, which my boy shares with me, staining my mouth with oil. I sit with him in the dark through every flashing, mesmerizing scene. A red-eyed robot topples skyscrapers like building blocks as people run in every direction. Ben squeezes my paw and chews his lip. Just when it seems the robot tyrant is an unstoppable force of destruction, a crime-fighting superhero dog descends from the clouds to fend off the robot and save the town. Ben jolts to his feet, cheering with a dozen other children, and I slide off his lap into the bucket of popcorn. Greasy kernels cling to my fur for the remainder of the film.

In the car, I rest against the buckle of Ben's seat belt as he breathlessly relives the film. At home, Ben retells the story again for Mother, swinging me by one foot as he jets around the kitchen. He mimics the action from his favorite scenes, using my body as a prop. After dinner, Dad presents Ben with a box wrapped in crinkly paper. My boy unwraps it in a rush, rattles the room with his excited squeals, then tackles Dad in a hug. I am unable to see the contents from my slumped position on the couch, but I am familiar with the tradition of gift-giving and predict it's a new toy.

Mother procures scissors, and the item is released from its zip-tie prison. Ben removes it with restrained reverence; it is the protagonist from the film—the canine superhero, adorned with a glimmering red cape and a flashy collar. The pup boasts of smooth, sleek fur, unmarked by time and off-screen adventure. Ben's infectious joy lingers in the air long after he has disappeared into his room. His muffled voice wafts down the hall, where I catch snippets of a story unfolding—a criminal's malicious plans are thwarted by the witty dog with supernatural speed and strength. His happiness lulls me into contentment.

But my contentment distorts into dis-ease when dusk transforms the living room wall into a grid of shadows, signaling the day's end. Where is my boy? The house has gone silent—no footsteps, no bristles against teeth, no small voice begging for five more minutes or a glass of water— only the steady hum of aging appliances. The shadows fall lower until they disappear into the dark woodgrain of the floor. Still, no one comes for me.

Morning comes, and I wake up alone for the first time since before Ben's birth, where I had waited, nestled in a bag of crisp tissue paper with a bow around my neck, anticipating the moment I would meet my child—my boy, Ben. My fur was a vibrant chestnut then, soft and full. I'd be unrecognizable now—a tangled mass of jaundiced beige, but I wouldn't trade a single day with Ben to return to my former glory. I will be remembered by my boy long after I've been worn down to nothing. Our time together will survive in his heart even when I've disintegrated into synthetic tufts.

However, right now, my limbs are splayed out on this stiff sofa in the same position they were when Ben tossed me here the day before. It seems my boy has forgotten about me.

A dripping sound from the kitchen—Mother is awake now. She shuffles into the room with a steaming mug and settles onto the cushion next to me. Her lips hover near the ceramic rim. Purple half-moons frame her tired eyes. Finally noticing my presence, she situates me upright against a pillow. Her touch warms my patchy fur, and I long to be held. I miss my boy.

The day passes as any other. My boy, with his boundless energy, zips from one activity to another—from breakfast and story time to soccer and playdates—but I remain unnoticed in the novelty of his recent gift. Rather than carrying *me* under his arm or nuzzling *me* against his pillowy cheek, he chooses the movie star pup for companionship. But I try not to mind; my boy is happy, and that pleases me.

Eventually, Mother carries me back to Ben's room and lays me gently on his bed, where I sit and wait for my boy to come back to me.

Sometime later, I hear rowdy footsteps echoing down the hall. A herd of boys bursts into the room, where Ben and his friends begin a frenzied search for fort-building supplies. The blanket on the bed is ripped out from under me and I am flung to the top of a dresser, where I slide across the surface and fall into a dark crevice between the dresser and the wall. Eventually, the chaos of the fort building calms, and the front door opens and closes as each friend returns home. I wait for my boy to come and find me, but night comes, and I remain wedged in the dark space, unseen.

Sunlight curves from the floor to the ceiling, then slips away entirely with the passing of each day. I've lost count of the cycles of light—the days passed since I last breathed my boy's familiar scent and felt his small hands tangled in my fur. I hear him rustling in the night—so close but impossibly out of reach. I wonder if the caped dog is making Ben happy—if he enjoys Ben's elaborate games and stories; if he is keeping bad dreams at bay.

My body has grown dry and stiff, flattened between this dresser and the wall. My hard nose scrapes the paint, and I've memorized every fleck and bump in the wall's texture. The trajectory of sunlight shifts, and the nights come quicker, the air grows cooler. I treasure the sounds of my boy in his room, crafting new worlds and imagining grand adventures. His sweet voice is like music, and in the stillest hours of night, I can just hear his steady breathing.

Some toys have never known love, and so I count myself among the lucky ones. I have known the love of the most beautiful soul—was there for him when his hands were too small and clumsy to even hold me. I watched his murky eyes change into the deep pools of electric blue they are today. I've heard his every cry, witnessed the spectrum of his complex emotions, and felt the radiance of his bright, pure spirit. If anything, I am grateful. My deep sadness comes only from knowing how much more there is to see and learn about my beautiful boy and how distant I am from any of it.

I lay unmoving, reflecting on my full life like I have every day since my fall, and I listen to the lively sounds of my boy romping around his room. But I am startled from my musings when something bumps the dresser and causes a loud crash. In the narrow crack of light, I see shards of glass littering the floor and the edge of a lampshade lying on its side.

Ben calls out, and soon I hear Mother's footsteps. Broom bristles scrape against the shattered glass, then a vacuum roars to life, clearing the sharp slivers.

Then I hear wood scraping against wood. Light floods the darkness, and my body falls and thuds against the floor. A fragment of milky glass snags my fur, but I don't mind.

Because I can see my boy. And he sees me.

Tears well in his electric blue eyes, and every white tooth gleams when he smiles.

Mother carefully plucks the piece from my fur and inspects me all over before handing me to my boy.

Ben embraces my limp body, and I hear his wild heartbeat in his chest. I hope he never lets go. His cheeks are warm and soft against my hard nose, and he smells like sunshine and bubble gum toothpaste.

I can see my old playtime friends lying on the rug. They acknowledge my return with smiling faces. And at their center, that movie star hero-dog sits with his red cape and flashy collar. My boy sets me down and kneels before the dog, and for a moment, time stands still.

I've been gone too long. Of course, he's replaced me. When he needed a friend, I was nowhere to be found. I wasn't there for him.

But then, he removes the canine hero's iconic accessory, that glimmering red cape, and fastens it around my thin, scruffy neck. And I feel like the bear in the gift bag all those years ago—sleek and new, with a lifetime of love to give to my child—my boy, Ben.

My paws lift as my boy scoops me up, and together we race through every room, soaring as one. My boy's warm hands feel larger, and his eyes seem older, but I know his love for me hasn't changed; it's the kind of love that lasts a lifetime.

Friends Don't Let Friends Eat Poison

A friendship develops between two species as they bond over food.

"I wouldn't eat that if I were you."

Bender slowly raised his head above the rim of the garbage can and looked for the source of the voice. "Who's there?"

Rix leaned against the cinderblock wall, his shadowed face half illuminated by the flickering lights. He scanned the parking lot before crossing to where Bender stood frozen, elbow-deep in the open dumpster. In one meaty paw, he held a half-eaten honey bun, its fatty glaze congealing in the heat of the summer night.

Rix sidestepped a pothole swirling with oil and surveyed the mess Bender had created. Trash bags lay ripped open on the asphalt, flies buzzed greedily over the piles of waste. Bender's eyes shifted between the stranger and the empty parking lot as he stooped to collect more dumpster delicacies in his arms. Rix shook his head and sighed. "Seriously, man, that stuff is disgusting." He lowered his voice. "And you're making such a mess over here; you're going to attract the hoomans."

Bender smashed the remainder of the pastry in his mouth, crystalized sugar crusting his muzzle. "Just leave me alone; I know what I'm—"

Headlights pierced the dark gas station lot and beamed over the shadowed corner where the bear and the racoon stood. Rix darted beneath a heap of trash, and Bender lumbered behind the metal dumpster. When all was quiet again, Rix hissed, "Look, just trust me, this stuff is going to make you slow and fat...*ter*," he added, eyebrow raised at Bender's rump. "Not to mention what it will do to your fur."

The bear sat with an *oomph* and struggled with the packaging of another snack, claws clicking against each other. "So, you're telling me you never eat at these places? I find that hard to believe." He held the bag close to his eyes, concentrating. "Convenient, easy, and the hoomans don't bother you back here. What more could you want?" When Bender finally ripped open the bag, a few dusty potato chips flew to the ground.

Rix jabbed a thumb toward the squat building and rusty pumps. "Are you talking about the gas station? This, my friend, is no eatery."

Crunch, crunch, crunch.

"Works for me," Bender said, the line of drool oozing from his mouth an unnatural shade of orange.

Rix jumped up onto Bender's knee and swatted the bag out of his hand. He waved a spindly finger in the bear's face. "What's wrong with you? Have you *never* heard of preservinatives? Or partially hydro-urinated oils?"

Bender's eyes widened. "Uh, no."

Rix continued. "What about Trans-fat? Or high frootloops corn syrup, hm? Know what those are?"

Bender clicked his claws together, his shoulders hunched. "No, I don't. What are they?"

Rix stared up the bear's long, brown snout. "Poison," he whispered.

Bender gulped. "Poison? But—but this is hooman food. Why would hoomans eat poison?"

Rix scratched behind his ear. "It's because they like wrappers, my friend. That crinkly sound you hear?" Rix gestured to the chip bag lying on the ground. "Hoomans can't resist it. But the crinkly food is bad stuff, my man." The racoon crossed his wiry arms. "You ever wonder why hoomans are so lumpy and hairless?"

Bender leaned in closer. "Yeah, I guess I do wonder about that."

"Poison," Rix sniffed.

"Oh my," said Bender.

"And you know why they are so *slow*, always riding around in their ottermobiles?" Their wet noses almost touched. "It's because they eat so much poison that they can't hardly walk anymore," Rix said, emphasizing each word.

Bender clutched his chest. He sat back, thinking for a moment, then he rose and started to pace. "Hoomans sure are lumpy–and hairless; you're right about that." He turned to Rix, "but I've seen some fast ones before—you know, the road hoomans."

Rix waggled an eyebrow, "the road hoomans?"

"Yeah," said Bender, "the ones that run on the roads, breathing all heavy–kind of wet looking."

Rix considered this. "Ah yes, the runarounders." He turned to Bender, excitement in his voice. "That's the thing—the runarounders don't eat the crinkly food. That's how they are so fast—they don't eat poison from places like this." He waved a hand at the dumpster.

Bender frowned, "oh yeah? How do you know?"

Rix licked his palm and slicked back his fur. "I've been doing this a long time, pal. Let me show you where the runarounders eat."

***

The black night sky was beginning to soften, deep orange glowed in the East. Birds chirped, announcing to the mountain town it was morning.

A clatter echoed across the empty parking lot as a young man pushed a line of shopping carts into the store. Bender and Rix watched from the wooded hill. Rix made a sweeping motion with his hands like he was painting a rainbow. "Welcome to Hole Foods."

Bender stared slack-jawed. "Wow. This place is huge!" He pointed at the worker with the shopping carts. "What are those things?"

Rix squinted into the darkness. "Those are cages. That's so their food doesn't escape before the hoomans can put it in their ottermobiles," Rix said. He jabbed Bender's round belly with an elbow. "Come on, follow me."

The grocery store parking lot was dimly lit, the sunrise taking its time. Rix skittered around the building, and Bender lagged behind him. A succession of beeps rang out as a boxy white truck rolled backwards toward a large opening at the back of the store.

"Oh, this will be a piece of cake." Rix rubbed his palms together.

"What do you mean? Is there cake in that thing?" Bender licked his lips. Rix ignored the question and gestured to the man opening the back of the truck. His head bobbed up and down to whatever was coming from the plushy device curved around his skull.

Rix pointed at the man. "That one's called Duh Mass." He smirked, proud of his vast knowledge of the hoomans. "He won't notice us. One time he didn't even notice that his ottermobile was driving away without him, doors hanging open and everything." Rix chuckled at the memory. "Good old, Duh Mass."

Bender's eyes grew big. "You know him?"

"No," Rix said, "I just know that's what the other hoomans call him. They all have names for each other." He focused on the man, who was now standing inside the truck, spinning in circles, and moving his mouth.

"What's wrong with him? Do you think he has rabies?" Bender asked, scratching his armpit. The man started jerking his body in strange, repetitive motions.

Rix replied, "It's the head device." He cupped his fingers around his eyes and leaned closer, watching. "It controls their bodies, but they seem to like it." The man stopped swaying and resumed the task of moving boxes and crates off the truck and into the building. Rix's voice grew serious, "Okay, you stay right here. I'll be back." He bounded from their hiding spot and snuck toward the truck before Bender could protest.

Bender waited, nervously twisting a patch of fur, until finally, Rix ducked under the truck and tip toed back to the anxious bear. A strand of sausages hung around his neck like a scarf, and he had a cluster of bananas wedged under each arm. He dropped his armload of goods in front of Bender, who touched each item reverently.

"Great Grizzly, this looks amazing."

Rix reached for a large tin canister and peeled back the lid. "Here buddy, you've got to try some of this; you're going to love it." Rix grabbed a clammy handful of aromatic black dust and licked it.

Bender peered into the tin. His shoulders drooped. "That's dirt."

"Oh no, big boy. This is orgasmic fair trade Guatemalan light roast coffee." Rix planted his face into the tin and inhaled. "With notes of citrus," his voice echoed.

Bender grabbed the can and shook, grounds tumbling into his open mouth. He chewed, a dry crunching sound, and nodded his approval. "I like it." He coughed a spray of coffee dust, then pointed to an oblong purple object that had rolled away from the pile. "What's that one?"

Grabbing it with both paws, Rix shook it near his ears. "This one's an eggplant." He handed it to Bender, who imitated the action.

"Are there eggs in it?" the bear asked.

Rix bit a chunk out of the side. "Only egg seeds. See?"

He speared one with a sharp claw. "You've got to plant them first. It takes a long time though."

"I see," Bender said, taking in all the new information.

A rattling of keys alerted Rix to the loading dock. He began gathering the grocery items, pushing some into Bender's arms. "What's going on?" Bender asked.

"Time to go. That's Jer Koff." Bender waited for an explanation. Rix huffed. "He has superior intelligence and always knows when food is missing. And he won't be very happy about it." He waved his arm, urging Bender to move faster. "Looks like we'll be taking our meal to-go today, brother."

The two disappeared behind the dumpsters and into the woods, alive with the thrill of a successful heist—and too much caffeine.

***

"I wouldn't eat that if I were you."

Frightened, the scruffy opossum jumped a foot into the air, dropping his bag of M&Ms. They rolled across the uneven pavement and landed at the feet of an unusually lean bear propped against the gas station dumpster.

Bender chuckled. "Have you never heard of preservinatives, my friend?"

Storage Unit Purgatory

A group of old friends are beginning to feel increasingly irrelevant.

"Zenith, do you believe in life after storage?" Baldwin asked, breaking the long-held silence in the climate-controlled unit of the Stow-and-Go storage facility.

Zenith grouched, "Are we really having this conversation again?" His voice echoed off the slick wood of Baldwin's grand surface. "Why don't you ask Singer, she's much wiser. And older. Aren't you, Singer?"

"A lady never reveals her age," Singer replied. "I may be your elder, but I'm far too pragmatic to dwell on such abstract notions. And besides, if any of us were to possess an understanding of the world's inner workings, it would be you. You've been privy to all kinds of speeches and sermons and what have you. I'm sure you can muster up an answer for the boy."

Zenith griped, "The kid doesn't like my answers. I've told him before; we're here as long as we're needed or until we break down, and then we're through. Simple as that."

Baldwin whined, "But don't you ever think about what comes next? We aren't broken; we could still serve a purpose, right?"

"Maybe *you*, kid."

"No, I mean all of us! Zenith, you used to bring people

together—make them laugh and dance, and Singer, you brought simplicity and ease into peoples' lives. Remember?" Neither responded. "It's just hard for me to believe that this is it—that this is where it ends."

"Look kid, life isn't always parties and jigs," Zenith grated. "Sometimes you're the center of the fun, sometimes you're the bearer of bad news, and sometimes you're just a bulky box of wood for folks to set their cocktails on."

Singer coughed. "Sounds like someone has a bit of dust on his dial."

"Says the bitter old woman who mended long johns for a living," Zenith grumbled.

"I'll have you know, I have assisted in creating some of the century's most sophisticated styles." Singer carried on. "I've got more *accomplishment* in one bobbin than you in your entire circuit board. I've clothed everyone from bitty babies and schoolboys to film stars and diplomats, you big block of wires."

"Oh yeah? Well, I've broadcast famous speeches of presidents, prime ministers, and the Queen of England herself! Have you ever filled a room with the voice of a monarch?"

Singer huffed.

"I thought not," said Zenith.

"Guys, guys, it's obvious you've both accomplished some amazing things, and I'm truly honored to be stored in the same unit as such heroes as yourselves."

Zenith's small glass dome gleamed, and Singer dipped

her cast-iron pedal politely.

Baldwin continued, "But I just can't accept that we're no longer needed, that we've become irrelevant. We're made to do more than just sit around and look shiny." Baldwin's voice dropped to a low C. "I know the world is changing, but this can't be it for us."

Zenith and Singer exchanged knowing looks.

"I know this is difficult for you, dear," Singer spoke softly. "I imagine you miss being a source of pleasure for others and that this place must be quite dull for such a jovial fellow as yourself, but I like to believe that pleasure will never become irrelevant." Her rusting wheel turned slowly. "I've seen a lot in my many years of service, and even in the worst of times, well, especially in the worst of times, people want to feel happy. And you, boy, are gifted in bringing happiness to others. Don't you forget it."

Baldwin clinked gratefully, his mellow voice echoing in the dark unit. "I hope you're right, Singer. I just feel like I have so much left to give—like I'm not fulfilling my purpose here. And more than anything, I just miss being *touched*—by the clumsy beginners, the prodigies, the teachers, anyone. It was always the greatest feeling."

"I know it well, dear."

Zenith coughed in his corner. He wasn't the most tactile or emotional, instrument.

"Zenith," Singer cooed, "I know we weren't always situated on the same floor of The House, but I could always hear you from my sunny corner upstairs."

147

"You used to be pretty loud yourself."

"I'll accept that as acknowledgment of my productivity. Thank you, sir." She continued. "As I was saying, I seem to recall hearing the music of an exceptionally jaunty performer, though his name eludes me. Luke Wellington? Drew Evenson? Oh, it's right on the tip of my needle."

"Duke Ellington! Oh yes, my speakers made his music sound real crisp, like the band was right there in the room." Zenith said. "Those were the good days."

"They certainly were. And I would bet my foot pedal that an appliance as fine as yourself could still broadcast such lively tunes with as crystal-clear quality as ever," Singer crooned.

"There may be a few knicks in my veneer," Zenith said, "but this transmitter's as strong as the day it was assembled." He paused. "Only problem is, I don't know if this old battery has any life left in it."

"Could you try?" Singer cajoled. "Even a minute of music would bring us all such joy."

"Oh yes," Baldwin added, "it would be a real treat, Zenith."

"Alright, alright, just hold your horses now. Let's see what I can do." Zenith stretched his antenna and twisted his dial, searching through garbled static for that old, familiar sound. "I've got a signal, but it's weak."

"You can do it, Zenith," Baldwin chanted.

Snippets of conversation warbled through the iron speaker grate, maybe a ball game or a talk show. When he caught the faintest hint of a musical instrument, Zenith froze. "I think I've got something!" The sound grew louder, and the others paused, listening intently to the pulsating, metallic screeches emitting from Zenith's speaker.

"What in the name of Christmas morning is this ruckus?" Singer choked. "Oh, turn it off, turn it off!"

"Hold on, hold on." Zenith searched for another station.

Baldwin shared Singer's distaste. "I have to agree; that was just terrible."

Zenith worked intensely for the next few minutes, moving his dial a hair's width from one tick to the next, passing static or equally horrifying musical performances.

Singer heard it first. "Go back, go back!"

Zenith eased the dial counterclockwise, and suddenly, the room filled with the sounds of life—a brassy saxophone, a lazy trombone, and a passionate violin mimicking the vocalist's melody.

"Oh, this takes me back," Singer cried. "Doesn't it make you want to dance, Zenith? Zenith?"

Zenith was humming along in his gravelly baritone, caught up in an era long since passed.

"Man, this sounds great," said Baldwin. "Can you turn it up?"

The volume intensified; the group was in a trance. Singer, trapped in memories of her golden years, Zenith transported to a time of new beginnings, and Baldwin, enraptured by the music's joy and lightness.

Then, without warning, the sound choked and sputtered, and silence cloaked the room once again. For a moment, no one spoke, but each knew how disappointed the other must be.

Singer sighed, "well, it was lovely while it lasted. Thank you, Zenith."

But Zenith only grunted.

The air felt charged, like a remnant of the music lingered in the darkness. They fell into the silence they knew so well, settling into storage unit purgatory with fresh resignation. Somewhere, an air conditioner hummed, blowing its cool gusts into the stagnant room. Even Baldwin had run out of things to say.

Then, like a whisper, Baldwin pulled his ivory keys to himself and broke the silence with a soft chord, its cheerful sound in stark contrast to the dejected spirit of the unit. He played another, then another, growing in volume and speed until he had perfectly matched the sound and style of the piano just heard in the radio performance. He let the chords loop while he picked out the melody on the right half of the keys.

Singer's pedal tapped to the beat. Zenith's dial dipped left and right.

The unit came alive with the sound of Baldwin's playing. He captured the nostalgia, the energy of the song, and for a moment, he felt a sense of rightness—purpose, fulfillment. As he brought the song to an end, hope lingered in the air with the final note.

And as the note died out, something clinked and chimed at the front of the unit—keys jangling against a lock. Voices. Singer nearly rolled with surprise when the steel door lifted, and sunlight flooded the darkness. Two men stood at the entrance scratching their heads. One carried a file on a clipboard, consulting the pages as the other man stepped inside and began looking around, searching behind boxes, and peeking beneath Baldwin's underside.

"I must be hearing things. There's no one in here, and it doesn't look like anything's been touched," the man said. "Just a bunch of dusty old stuff."

The other man lifted a page from his clipboard. "Check the security footage, just to be certain." He squinted at the paper, scratching his head. "Hmm, I don't know how this one slipped under the radar, but oddly enough, it looks like the owner has missed quite a few payments. We're going to need to get in contact with them." He looked up and gazed around at the antiques, frozen in time in a cement storage facility. "Alright, lock her up."

***

The steel door rolled up, and sunlight flooded the darkness. A woman stood at the entrance, silhouetted by the blinding daylight. Before her, another figure sat in a wheelchair, and together they maneuvered into the unit.

Singer nearly snapped her needle. "Zenith, Baldwin—it's the Little Master! He's come back for us! Oh, and he's quite grown up."

Zenith felt a jolt in his oscillator coil. Baldwin's strings tingled under his soundboard.

The two stepped out of the shadows and into the dim light of the storage unit. The old man's voice was thin and raspy as he struggled to rise from the chair. "Hello, old friends."

The young woman, wearing a monochromatic uniform of light blue, a nametag, and white sneakers, assisted him through the tunnel of stacked belongings. The old man reached out a skeletal hand, touching each item he passed. He caressed the rounded, black surface of Singer's cast iron body. He followed the slope of Zenith's bulky frame, his skin making a papery sound against the dry wood. When he came to Baldwin, he shuffled around the miscellaneous stacks and lowered himself onto the bench tucked beneath the row of ebony and ivory. He brushed his fingers along the length of keys as his companion stood behind, bracing his frail shoulders. And then, he began to play.

Baldwin sighed at the sound that reverberated from his diaphragm when the Little Master trailed his fingers along the keys in a spidery accent. The sound was rich, classic— the masterpiece of some great, long-dead composer. The old man's shoulder blades jutted from his back like the sharp peaks of furniture beneath a thin dust sheet. His hands trembled, but his fingers held fast and hit each note with precision and strength. He closed his eyes and let the music wash over him, carry him away to another world—one of vitality, of independence.

The woman dabbed at the moisture in her eyes as the old man brought the song to a close. She guided him around the bench and back through the maze of boxes to the wheelchair waiting at the entrance. Seated once again, the man gazed softly at the summation of generations of belongings.

"Goodbye, old friends."

***

"Zenith, what does *auction* mean?" Baldwin asked, listening to the voices from the crowd gathered just beyond the closed door of unit 715 of the Stow-and-Go storage facility.

"It's where they cart you off to the clown with the most money," Zenith said.

"Well, seems like someone has a kink in his coils," Singer interjected. "Don't be so negative, Zenith. The boy asked a simple question. Baldwin, an auction is an opportunity for us to go to new homes, to be purchased by someone who finds us to be of particular interest."

"But, what about the Little Master? Why can't we go home with him?"

"I know it's hard to understand," Singer sighed, "but sometimes we outlive our masters. Outlive our usefulness to the ones we've served."

"I'm sure going to miss him."

"We all are, dear. But we'll always hold the memory of him and all the masters before him, deep within our parts. We don't forget."

"I'd like to forget this terrible storage unit," Zenith grumbled.

"Oh, come on now, Zenith, you know you'll miss us." Baldwin said, "I know I sure will. Besides, I don't know how I can ever go on without your *good vibrations*."

"No, no, no," Zenith said. "Not that song again, please no."

"What was that? Play it again, you said?" Baldwin jested.

"Yes, that's certainly what I heard," Singer joined in.

"Quiet you two; it's starting," Zenith said.

The auctioneer began. "Good afternoon, ladies and gentlemen. I'd say we've got some real beauties in this unit here today."

"Here that, Zenith? He thinks you're beautiful," Baldwin whispered.

"Quiet!" Zenith hissed.

"Let's start the bidding at one hundred dollars. Can I get a hundred? $100 there in the back. Can I get $150, $150?"

Zenith grumbled, "This is humiliating."

"It will be over soon," said Singer.

"I'm really going to miss you guys," said Baldwin.

"$700, can I get $700?"

"Baldwin, don't you know how these things work?" Singer asked.

"A thousand dollars folks; someone give me $1,000."

"No, not really," Baldwin said.

"The highest bidder will receive the whole unit–all of us."

Baldwin's black wood glinted. "You don't say?"

"$5,000 and SOLD to the young man in the back."

"Did he just say 5,000?" Zenith asked.

"Sounded like it to me," said Baldwin.

After a while, the chatter quieted down and the metal

doors lifted, and sunlight flooded the darkness. A young man strode toward the unit, sliding his checkbook back into his pocket.

"Say, Zenith," Singer said. "That man. I may be going mad, but who does he remind you of?"

Zenith paused, dial wavering. "He reminds me of The Little Master."

A moment passed between them before Baldwin asked, "Zenith, do you believe in life after storage?"

"I'm starting to, kid."

How I Came to Leave Hartfield Manor

A nursery maid cares deeply for her young charges, but is it time for her to move on?

I never thought I'd leave Hartfield Manor, but the train is moving now, and there is no going back. Everything I hold dear is stowed beneath my seat or in a bundle on my lap; I took only what I needed to start over. I shall miss the staff and little Peter and the twins, but they'll all forget me soon enough. Once they've hired a new nursery maid, I'll become a distant memory. Lord Thorne will probably fabricate a tale to besmirch my good name—something about how I was a fraud or a danger to his children, but they will grow up someday and see what true dysfunction lies behind those stone walls, and they won't begrudge my leaving. They'll understand then.

It wasn't always this way.

Years ago, when I first arrived at Hartfield Manor, with little more than a carpet bag and letter of reference from the academy, I was enamored with its grandness, the beautiful gardens, and the air of importance I felt the moment I stepped inside. My personal quarters, adjacent to the nursery, were spacious with tall, East-facing windows, and I couldn't have been more pleased. I was soon introduced to my new charges, the young twins, misses Katherine and

Margaret. They were so small then and hardly speaking–shy little things hiding themselves behind their mother's skirts. I gifted each of them a peppermint candy, which they swiftly consumed, and we became fast friends.

My mistress, Lady Thorne, was a bright, amiable woman, and I liked her immediately. She spoke kindly to me, and we fell into an easy companionship of sorts, as much as one could with their superior. Shortly after I was taken on, she disclosed to me that she was again with child and though elated with the news, felt quite ill most days. But when she was not too indisposed, she'd come to the garden and sit beside me as we watched the girls play in the grass. They'd bring us wilted flowers in their sticky hands, and Lady Thorne would pretend they were bouquets fit for a queen, tucking them into her hair or dress. The girls would gaze wide-eyed at their mother and cover her cheeks in kisses, as adoring of her charm and beauty as the rest of us were.

Those were my most cherished days at Hartfield Manor. Mr. Thorne traveled often and for long stints of time, so whenever he returned, the house behaved like it was a holiday and put together a grand spread for dinner. Lady Thorne especially anticipated her husband's return, giving special attention to her attire and toilette on those nights. Adorned in gems and shimmering satin, she looked every bit a duchess, even being heavy with child. On her way down to dinner, she would always stop by the nursery to kiss the girls goodnight. Katherine and Margaret would beg their mother for a song, and she always obliged, her voice high and clear, luring them into slumber. Her perfume lingered in the air as the children drifted off, contented smiles on their cherubic faces.

As the time came and Lady Thorne gave birth to their third child, a son they named Peter, the spirit shifted in the house. Peter was an inconsolable infant; his face always screwed up in the most displeased pout. He screeched and bellowed, such volume from one so small. But Lady Thorne was delighted with him and determined to meet his needs and nurse him herself, ignoring Lord Thorne's insistence on the impropriety of it, but, regardless, little Peter would not take to her, and she grew increasingly rattled by his cries and disturbed by her own exhaustion. His constant wailing unsettled everyone. A seasoned wet nurse was finally dispatched, and the house resumed a modicum of normalcy.

Peter cried more than he smiled, but he was mollified by the outdoors, and so I spent many hours pushing him in his pram until the arches of my feet ached. On warm days I would set out with the girls on either side and Peter in his pram, and we'd visit the pond, where frogs and ducks and all manner of creatures buzzed and scuttled across the glassy surface. I'd let the twins strip off their shoes and dip their toes in the cool water. They'd rip the seeds from cattails and toss them into the wind, where the breeze would blow them right back into their hair. It was wonderful entertainment.

When Peter began to fuss, I'd take him out and bounce him on my hip. He'd reach for the ribbons in my hat and coo and gurgle as I pulled my head away, or he'd cover my cheeks in sloppy baby kisses. I remember a certain occasion when I turned to the house and saw Lady Thorne watching us from the window, her pale hands pressed against the glass. I'd called to the girls and told them to wave, but Lady

Thorne had disappeared from view when we turned back.

Before Peter was half a year old, Lady Thorne announced she was expecting again. Everyone was surprised, though she wore a smile when she shared the news. The time passed slowly, with Lady Thorne remaining in her rooms more as the months progressed. When she did come to the nursery to visit the children and read them books or play silly games, they would all fight for a spot on her lap, wiggling their way into her arms and struggling to find room against her growing belly. She'd smooth the girls' hair and tickle Peter under his chubby chin, then all too soon, she'd bid them goodbye and shuffle back to her room, too tired for much else. On the rare occasion both Lord and Lady Thorne came to the nursery together, it was a most special treat for the children, and for me, as I was temporarily reprieved from my duties while they enjoyed the intimate family time.

Lord and Lady Thorne were an amicable couple. I never witnessed a dispute or disagreement between them until I happened upon them one early morning, rushing through the foyer as I was just leaving. A footman was carrying Lord Thorne's cases outside to a waiting coach as Lady Thorne trailed behind, begging her husband to postpone the matter of business that was calling him away. Worry lines creased her forehead as she spoke in rushed whispers. She told him she'd been feeling unusual and didn't want to be left alone in her state, but he kissed her cheek and assured her he would be swift and efficient, then took his leave. From my shadowed alcove, I heard her heavy footsteps go up the staircase, down the hall, and into her room, where she slammed the door shut. Then a sound, like ceramic shattering against wood, rang through the halls, and I darted away before I became the next target.

I kept the children busy that day and out of the way. We poked around the kitchen, where Mrs. Findlay patiently showed the girls how to make bread. She gave them each a ball of dough and let them knead it into lumpy patties with their clumsy palms. They managed to coat all of us in flour, even little Peter, who sat munching a biscuit, watching the activity with busy eyes.

On our way out of the kitchen, we nearly collided with Mr. Conrad, the Butler, who was rather fond of the children, never having had any of his own, and he showed the girls the wall of bells in the servants' hall, how each one corresponded to different rooms throughout the house. The bells reminded the girls of Christmas, and they sang carols all the way back up the stairs and into the nursery. That night, after I had put the children to sleep and retired to my room, I heard heavy footsteps and the squealing voices of the maids running through the halls, followed by frantic instructions from Mrs. Pellum, the housekeeper, urging them to move quickly and be calm.

When I caught up to her and asked what the matter was, the older woman wrung her hands and urged me to pray, saying that Lady Thorne was unwell, and the doctor was on his way. None of us slept that night, as we could hear her cries echoing off the walls and felt the acute chill of dread they carried. When the night had nearly turned to morning, and the doctor had packed his case and left, Lady Thorne's maid recounted what had happened, and everyone in the servants' hall listened in silence. It was a girl, she told us, strange and small, born with tufts of auburn hair but no color in her cheeks, no cry on her lips. The old housekeeper sobbed, and Mr. Conrad's fists turned white before he turned and shut himself in his office.

We all wore mourning clothes for several weeks, Lord Thorne a few months, and I dressed the girls in gray woolen frocks trimmed in black, but after that night, I never saw Lady Thorne in color again. The winter passed in a long, dreary slur of cold days and cloudy skies.

Whenever he was home, Lord Thorne would stop in to see the children, remarking on how much they'd all grown. He'd bring them trinkets from his travels—miniature sailboats and dolls with marble eyes—and they loved him for it. We saw less of Lady Thorne and rarely the two of them together.

In Spring, when everything was green again, the children and I made a visit to the seaside one afternoon, where the girls searched for shells in the wet, cool sand. Peter sat by the shore, grabbing fat handfuls of sand and trying more than once to consume it. When we returned home, the girls looped twine through their favorite shells and made necklaces—one for me and one for their mother. We brought hers to her room, and she smiled as they placed it over her head, praising their handiwork, but her face did not shine as it used to, and her eyes held a coolness when they flitted to the shells around my own neck.

In Autumn, Lord Thorne announced that it was time for the girls to begin their studies, and he employed a governess, a highly recommended Miss Mary Weston. The children and I had waited on the steps to greet her on the day of her arrival, and when she stepped out of the coach in a garish feathered hat, she stared up at the expanse of Hartfield Manor with a cattish smile. She was young, not much older than myself, with sharp, striking features. I extended my hand to her, and as she grasped mine, she looked at me down the bridge of her pert nose and said, "what a pleasure it is to meet you," dragging out the word *pleasure* as if it caused her pain. She eyed the girls from head to toe, then reached out and pinched their round cheeks. "I see I shall have to incorporate lessons in self-restraint and the wiles of over-indulgence." Then she strode past us and into the house.

The girls studied under her stringent tutelage from morning until lunchtime, and I relished the quiet hours with little Peter, who'd finally outgrown his troubled infancy. He was a cautious, sensitive boy, easily agitated by his gregarious sisters, but he thrived during our mornings together. We'd hunt for bugs in the garden, and he'd watch me closely as I pointed at all the things we saw, giving them a name. *Tree. Flower. Bird.* When he repeated the words back to me, my heart swelled with affection and pride as if he were my own child, bridging our worlds with his acquisition of language.

As we settled into our new rhythm, Lord Thorne took on various duties which kept him home more, and he developed an interest in the girls' education, often popping in and standing at the back of the room as Miss Weston tutored the girls in writing or arithmetic. Sometimes he'd already be in the study with Miss Weston when I brought the girls in for their morning classes. On one day in particular, we arrived a bit early, accidentally startling Lord Thorne and Miss Weston. The two had jumped apart from each other, flustered by our interruption. Lord Thorne appeared rumpled and disheveled, Miss Weston's hair mussed and slipping from its pins.

I smiled and greeted them both as I normally did, pretending I saw nothing, but I could not score the image of his wild eyes and heaving chest or her flushed neck from my mind.

It was soon after this that Lady Thorne called for me, and we took tea together in her sitting room. She was silent as I prattled on about the children, detailing how equally mischievous and marvelous they each were. She left her tea untouched, and with a faraway stare, finally informed me she was expecting another child. I was unable to conceal my shock and nearly spilled my tea on the settee. She did not smile. I took her hand and assured her it would be a wonderful child, vibrant and smart, just like its brother and sisters. She nodded, picking at the edge of a napkin, and dismissed me.

As Lady Thorne's waistline grew with her condition, so did Lord Thorne's boldness in his pursuit of Miss Weston. I was utterly convinced of their transgressions and heartbroken for my mistress, who passed the days in a queer state of despondence. One afternoon, I invited her to join the children and I for a picnic in hopes of coaxing her into the fresh air and lifting her spirits. The girls had been practicing a song for her, so Lady Thorne, still in her black mourning clothes, sat on a blanket as Katherine and Margaret took each other's hands and began to sing a tune of a young bird finding its wings and flying away.

Little Peter stood clapping along, trying to mimic the words as they sang. Lady Thorne smiled and held her arms out to him, but he turned away from her and dove against my chest. Her face fell, and her lips stiffened. As the song ended, the girls embraced their mother and settled beside her. Lady Thorne reached for Peter again and pulled him onto her lap, but he wailed and thrashed his arms about, cutting her across the lip with a jagged fingernail. She gasped, then reared back and struck him on the cheek, leaving a hot handprint on his pale skin.

Then she shot up, sending a plate of grapes rolling into the grass. "This is your doing!" She stabbed the air with a finger. "You've poisoned my own children against me." She spun on her heels and returned to the house in a flurry of black petticoats.

Peter cried against my shoulder until he fell asleep.

I avoided my mistress after that day and for many days after, but I was unable to avoid the ever-present Lord Thorne and Miss Weston. I was an accomplice, my silence only aiding in their illicit trysts, and it was robbing me of all peace. One afternoon, when Lord Thorne was away from the house, I came upon Miss Weston alone in the halls and approached her.

"You must stop this business with Thorne," I whispered. "Our mistress doesn't deserve this."

She raised a dark eyebrow and stepped closer. "Master Thorne says what his wife deserves is *the madhouse.*"

I nearly choked. "Lord Thorne would *never.* I refuse to believe that."

"Believe what you want," she leaned in and ran a finger down the side of my cheek. "I'm only telling you what the master himself told me this morning, *in his bedchamber*."

Heat flooded my face. "You will lose your position, Mary. You're playing a dangerous game."

"Me? My position is perfectly secure, but you, my dear, are quite replaceable. I'm sure there are hundreds of poor country girls like you that would crowd the gate to fill your position." She turned her back to me and began to walk away. "Now, run along, back to those pudgy little children."

And I did run—straight to Lady Thorne's door and into her chambers without so much as a knock, but inside the dark room, Lady Thorne lay asleep, undisturbed by my boisterous entrance. The mere sight of her evoked every memory of that terrible afternoon—her frightening outburst, her accusations against me, her handprint against Peter's face—and I fled back into the hallway, where I saw Miss Weston standing in the shadows, watching.

***

By month's end, Lady Thorne's birth pangs began, and the doctor was sent for. After a long, anxious night, we all sighed with relief when we heard the news: the child was born—a healthy baby girl with auburn hair and rosy cheeks. When I went in to visit Lady Thorne that morning and meet my newest ward, I found the babe had already been handed off to the wet nurse.

I knelt by Lady Thorne's side. "Congratulations, Ma'am; I hear she's a fine child. What is her name?"

But she did not answer me.

"Shall I bring her to you then, once she's been fed?"

Her voice was muffled against her pillow. "I don't care what you do with her. Just keep her away from me." She turned and said nothing else. I drew the curtains, further shrouding the room in darkness, and I left her to rest.

I found the babe in the nursery, already swaddled and sleeping in her bassinet. I caressed the infant's downy cheeks, her tiny nose, and when she opened those guileless eyes, a strange rush of affection swept over me; I couldn't tear myself away from her.

When her cries rattled the silent nights, I came to her. When she soiled her linens, I changed her. When she refused the call of sleep, I held her to myself and sang lullabies, swaying in the dark until her eyelids fluttered closed.

Within a few months of baby Victoria's birth, as she was eventually named, Lord Thorne called me into his study. I came promptly, passing Miss Weston in the hall just outside. She curled her lip at me as I opened the door and slipped inside. Lord Thorne remained seated at his desk as he informed me, with little ado, that my services at Hartfield Manor were no longer necessary. He did not look up from his papers. I was given generous severance, train fare, and one day to gather my belongings.

My heart broke when I bid farewell to Mr. Conrad, and Mrs. Pellum, and the servants, and then again three times over as I bid the children goodnight for the last time. I kissed them each on the cheek and hoped they wouldn't feel the wet tears on my own. I slipped from the house early the next morning, before anyone was awake, and caught the earliest train into the city.

***

That was several hours ago. Now, the train is finally lurching to a stop as it pulls into the station. Passengers stretch and reach for their bags as we all shuffle into the aisle. An elderly woman turns around and cranes her neck, staring at the bundle in my arms as we disembark.

"Was that wee little one here the whole time? He was such a quiet little fellow."

I smile and clutch baby Victoria tighter against my chest. "It's a girl."

A Tempestuous Mind

A troubled woman struggles to bring herself to a state of mindfulness.

I fear I am unwell.

My startling outburst last evening must have confirmed this for you, and it will come as no surprise to anyone if you choose to put me away. I hear the viscount committed his own wife for a much lesser offense; the poor woman allegedly exhibited a fit of rage over tangled embroidery thread. Describing her behavior as "unnerving and volatile," his assessment was damning enough to secure her future behind a stone-walled asylum. Though I dare never mention where my loyalties lie in the matter, I feel quite sympathetic toward the woman; needlework can be such a maddening affair.

You have assured me you'd never betray me in such a fashion, that you understand the nature of my weaker sex to be prone to fits of temperamental neuroticism, but I fear even you would be alarmed by the increasing pervasiveness of such *fits* into my well-being. I strain from the effort of concealing them from you, as I cannot bear the thought of you looking upon me with disdain or detachment. If you knew the depth of my unsettled mind, you would cast me away like a thorny weed. But I am, and shall ever be, your sweet-smelling rose, the pride of your garden. And so, I quell my agitation and stomp it into submission on this sandy shore.

It was you who first suggested I make these walks to the seaside to calm my nerves and quiet my disposition, but today, these fathomless waters have a rather un-soothing effect on me. I close my eyes and see myself as you must have last night, breathless, sobbing, unraveling—all in front of our dinner party of society's finest. I cannot express my humiliation or explain my behavior, as I do not quite understand it myself—though I am certain the viscount would attribute my distemper to possession of a demon and have me locked away indefinitely. I cannot make sense of the strangulating wave of fear and angst that came upon me so suddenly, as it so often does in moments of discomfort and stress, but I deeply regret ruining such an important evening for you—for everyone.

I will try not to ruminate over what they must be saying about me now; that I've grown mad, that I am a burden to you. I must be still and silence those thoughts. But the shrill squawking of seagulls reminds me of that gib-faced baroness's squeals and dashes any chance of me bridling my racing thoughts into docility. I am truly sorry that, in my episode of distress, I toppled her wine glass, but I am sure she will never forgive me for soiling her custom Parisian gown—though we might both agree it was a rather unflattering style.

Nevertheless, that haughty baroness will not consume my thoughts.

If you were here, you would find me in the remotest corner of this beach, my little sanctuary, where I've spread a quilt—a faithful companion on my worst days. I've secured my hat against the wind and high sun, but a gust whips at the blanket and lifts my skirts before I can tuck them under me. I adjust a wayward corner of the quilt, but the wind sends it back with a spray of white sand. Such insubordination from the elements today.

I sit here with eyes shut, breathing deeply, and I listen to the sea. It, too, listens to me. I wish it was as easy to speak frankly with you as it is to order my thoughts and unburden my heart to these waters.

Though I hope it is evident, that is, my undying devotion to you and our beloved children, I am becoming more desperate for these moments of respite from the bustling commotion of our estate. Some days, the thrill of being charged with the responsibilities of managing the household turns sour when I consider the likeliness of my failure—of making misguided decisions and plunging us into ruin or besmirching your good name. I am acutely aware of how my every action is weighed and judged, and above anything, I dread your disappointment in me. That weight looms like a heavy cloud.

The crashing of waves matches the rhythm of my chest, rising and falling. I taste salt in the air.

I am restless today.

More than my own fate, I worry about the futures of our children. I think of our son—a child who once believed I hung the moon now scoffs at my attention and turns away from my touch. The twins are ever their jovial selves, unfettered by anything but their Latin lessons. But the wee babe, though she is the only one who truly needs me, her cries pierce my constitution and wrack my restless slumber. I lay awake each night, waiting for her ragged wails to shatter the quiet. I lay awake, and I think of you. I dream of that endless summer when we were young and caught up in the throes of romance. You would meet me at the seaside with your boyish smile and a spray of roses bursting from your arms. Always white, like our Queen's wedding bouquet, though I doubt you'd remember.

My heart races as guilt trickles in. I've been away too long.

But I am not ready to return home to face you. I beg for strength from the air and the sea, but the sea is antagonizing me today.

I must compose myself.

I shall plant myself here until I've grown blissfully peaceful, too calm to consider my doubts and shortcomings or your disapproval. I won't think of our children, how they fill me with joy and exasperate me all within a single breath, how helpless I am when they are ill, how small I feel when they despise me. I will not succumb to exhaustion. I won't reflect on my duties as mistress, how the servants mock and disregard me. In the shadow of your steadfast strength, they see my weakness and insecurity, and the halls hiss with their whispers.

I have forgotten my steadied breathing and am now bent, plucking sand off the quilt, one glassy grain at a time. Though I recognize the futility of my actions, the effort soothes me. The sand settles into the seams of the thin, worn fabric. This quilt was once an impressive work of someone's painstaking craftsmanship—whose, I can't remember, but I've always been fond of it. Triangles and oblong shapes in all manner of colors and patterns fan out to form one magnificent starburst, an explosion of geometric jewel tones.

You would certainly laugh at me if you were here. I am lying on my stomach, letting my eyes roll over each shape, analyzing it for repetition, but each patch appears laid at random; there's one of emerald green, another with deep maroon flowers, and a blue patch with embroidered waves of golden wheat. The longer I stare, the more it appears the stalks are rising and falling, like they, too, are blowing in the wind. I blink away the illusion and exhale.

Be still.

This would be simple for you, or rather, you wouldn't find yourself with any need to be here at all. Thoughtful stillness requires no effort from you—you, crafted of elements utterly distinct from those which comprise me. So earthly, concrete, so quantifiable. You are guided by the laws of logic; your mind heeds your control. You would have never allowed yourself to exhibit such a public and undignified display of emotion.

I sit up, once again reliving the embarrassing scene. Cold perspiration gathers at my temples, and my heart quickens at the remembrance.

I once attempted to disclose details of my turbulent nature to you.

"Racing thoughts, what a notion," you'd said, genuinely humored by the imagery. But that humor has dissolved into fear behind your steely eyes, fear of the woman you've bound yourself to. And heavier than the weight of your disappointment is the thought that you might come to fear me. I will not hear of it. And so, I have come to accept that the landscape of my mind, so wild and untamed with its erratic weather and perpetual storms, is a place I must traverse alone.

A crab scuttles by, unperturbed by my inner turmoil. He wiggles himself down into the sand, nearly disappearing, and it strikes me how envious I am of this little crustacean, free to come and go as he pleases or to simply vanish altogether. Angry tears fall, unbidden.

Why am I so weak? How long until you realize my fragile dam has crumbled? 'Till you see how unsound I am and put me away? To shield your children from the mad woman they call "Mama"?

I unfasten my shoes in a rush, stride toward the shoreline, and heave one into the sea. It floats on the frothy wave for a moment, then fills with water and begins to sink.

A deluge of panic—*what have I done?*

You'll certainly know how unwound I am if I limp home wearing only one boot. What a stupid, stupid girl I am.

The waves accept my offering, and my rash decision is irrevocable. Sobs wrack me as I scream into the endless blue. I feel suffocated, my sobriety impaired by the chaos of my mind. Better the ocean takes me and drag me to its depths where no one can be touched by my madness.

I step into the cold, frothy edges when I hear a noise—a voice —rising above the one within that taunts me and urges me forward. Is it the sea? Does she welcome me with her watery embrace?

It calls again. The voice is behind me. Icy water licks at my ankles as I turn to the grassy hill beyond the sandy shore, where someone stands.

You, with your boyish smile and a spray of roses bursting from your arms. White roses. You call to me with arms outstretched. There is warmth in your expression.

Something brushes my leg in the frigid water.

My other shoe.

Acknowledgements

I am sincerely grateful to:

My husband, Brian, who has read every single iteration of these stories and never once yawned. You are infinitely giving and unfailing in your support. Thank you for pushing me to begin.

Russell Norman, an absolute gem. Thank you for seeing something in me and bringing your creative energy and vision to make this book possible. It's been *fun* every step of the way.

To Eric Bowles for your sharp eye for detail. This collection looks much shinier after you've come through and polished it up!

To the community of beautiful humans I've met through Reedsy and through Deidra Lovegren and Russell Norman, where I've found friends who often wear the superhero cape of "beta readers." (You all know who you are.) I appreciate your time and energy, and especially your honesty; friends don't let friends publish hot garbage.

About The Author

Aeris Walker hasn't taught at Harvard or written for The New York Times or worked as an editor for 20 years; she is a stay-at-home mother trying to finish her degree while chasing two kids around the house and begging them to put on pants.

A mother who, in her precious spare time, lets her imagination out for some fresh air and writes stories she hopes will resonate with her readers.

Aeris lives in North Carolina with her husband, young children, and a crotchety old dog.

You can find more information about Aeris Walker and her upcoming work at:

Blue Marble Publishing

bmpublish.com/aeris-walker/

Ingram Content Group UK Ltd.
Milton Keynes UK
UKHW022027290523
422506UK00014B/466